A

"*For All We Know* is a manifesto for all of those fascinated by the numinous realities posed by the UFO. Mike Fiorito finds the UFO in experiences as diverse as Catholic Mass to the modern rituals of heavy metal music and reveals a decentralized transcendence. A fun and extraordinary experience."

> — Dr. Diana Pasulka, Professor at the University of North Carolina Wilmington and Chair of the Department of Philosophy and Religion

"The UFO phenomenon is about many things, some of which can only be transmitted in the genre of fantastic literature, itself based on dreams, altered states, and out of body experiences. Mike Fiorito knows that and writes what he knows. Flying saucers appear alongside books, both of which appear alongside the so-called dead. "We are them." Take that as large and vast as you can.

> — Jeffrey J. Kripal, author of *The Flip: Epiphanies of Mind and the Future of Knowledge*. Dr. Kripal is also the J. Newton Rayzor Chair in Philosophy and Religious Thought at Rice University in Houston, Texas

"The best fiction transcends the genre to tell universal truths, and this is precisely what Fiorito has accomplished. *For All We Know* takes us on a journey to the greatest of unknowns—not only the world of the UFO, but ourselves and reality—revealing that, in order to understand the outer world, we must also turn inward."

> — Joshua Cutchin, author of *Ecology of Souls*

"What is so engaging about this marvelous mystical journey is that it encompasses the entirety of the post-entheogenic culture into a synthesized understanding of the soul incarnation into the multidimensional adventures of the mind. *For All We Know* is more than a read, it is an experience. While the book does more than describe other levels of awareness, we go through the machinations of consciousness of the protagonist Matteo and are transformed in the reading."

> — Alan Steinfeld, author of *Making Contact*

"*For All We Know* lies in Fiorito's sparse, evocative prose. In a series of short vignettes, he paints word pictures that delve into the experiences of a man's growing awareness of the world around him from his teen years in the mid-1970s through to his forties. It reminded me of the magical realism of writers such as Gabriel García Márquez and Jorge Borges, when quite suddenly mundane situations become imbued with the noetic and the extraordinary. I found the themes explored in this book to be powerfully relatable, from the musical references to the social commentary. A work I know I will return to again and again.

— Anthony Peake, author of *Cheating the Ferryman*

"For All We Know" takes the coming-of-age tale and reinvents it as a journey into the multifaceted universe of the unknown. Mike weaves aspects of the UFO phenomenon into the life experiences of Matteo. We follow Matteo's experiences in their full range from childhood to adulthood. Love, loss, music, psychedelics, and the questioning of reality are all aspects of life, as well as the UFO phenomenon. This is beautifully reflected in this book.

— Pricilla Stone, host of Quantum Wytch Cafe Podcast

"Fiorito's writing is so cinematic that I felt like I was there, right there in this powerful story. The idea that this is fiction or reality doesn't even matter because Fiorito succeeds in grabbing our attention and making us want more!"

— Marla Frees; author of *American Psychic* and practicing Consciousness Coach

"Fiorito's words act as the third eye, leading the reader to contemplate the larger picture from the paranormal to ufology studies into consciousness exploration."

— *Perceptions Today*

"Mike Fiorito's *For All We Know* is a literary excursion into the lived experience of the UFO phenomenon, interwoven into a tapestry of music, psychedelics and the flux-and-flow of everyday life. Written from the first-perspective the book provides the reader with a biographical snapshot of the processes by which anomalous experiences are perceived, processed and incorporated into a personal perspective on the cosmos and the human condition.'

— Dr. Jack Hunter is an anthropologist exploring the borderlands of consciousness, religion, ecology and the paranormal, and is author of *Ecology and Spirituality: A Brief Introduction*

FOR ALL WE KNOW
A UFO MANIFESTO

Mike Fiorito

Apprentice
House Press
Loyola University Maryland

First Edition

Library of Congress Control Number: requested

Hardcover ISBN: 978-1-62720-525-2
Paperback ISBN: 978-1-62720-526-9
Ebook ISBN: 978-1-62720-527-6

Cover Art by Pat Singer https://www.patsingerart.com/
Cover Design by Jack Stromberg
Promotional Development by Nathan McConarty
Editorial Development by MK Barnes

Published by Apprentice House Press

Apprentice
House Press
Loyola University Maryland

Loyola University Maryland
4501 N. Charles Street, Baltimore, MD 21210
410.617.5265
www.ApprenticeHouse.com
info@ApprenticeHouse.com

Dedicated to our future selves.

Contents

"Everything we call real is made of things that cannot be regarded as real." —Niels Bohr

"How does the living organism avoid decay? The obvious answer is: By eating, drinking, breathing and (in the case of plants) assimilating. The technical term is metabolism. The Greek word () means change or exchange. Exchange of what?" —Erwin Schrödinger

"To forget how to dig the earth and to tend the soil is to forget ourselves." —Mahatma Gandhi

A child said What is the grass?
fetching it to me with full hands
How could I answer the child?
I do not know what it is
any more than he.
—*Walt Whitman, "Song of Myself," from Leaves of Grass*

Every word or concept, clear as it may seem to be, has only a limit-ed range of applicability.
—*Werner Heisenberg*

"If you think you understand quantum mechanics, you don't un-derstand quantum mechanics."
—*Richard Feynman*

Preface

For All We Know is a spiritual fantasy that intricately depicts a series of deeply personal encounters interwoven with the enigmatic UFO phenomenon. In his youth, Matteo Tarquini becomes an eyewitness to an otherworldly vessel soaring across the New York City skyline. The awe-inspiring sight of the colossal, luminous craft traversing the night sky leaves a profound impact, simultaneously evoking both fear and fascination. The experience of witnessing an extraordinary extraterrestrial technology vanish into the depths of the cosmos at unimaginable speeds leaves an indelible mark on all who encounter it.

We follow Matteo as he finds solace in the sanctuary of his Catholic school, where the iconic imagery and music mesmerize him, transporting him to another realm akin to being lifted aloft in a UFO. In a later chapter, Matteo embarks on a mind-altering journey, partaking in an LSD experiment with a companion, pushing the boundaries of his human understanding. Through this transcendent encounter, he delves into the depths of the mysterious realities that potentially coexist alongside our everyday experiences. Matteo's path takes him from his rough-and-tumble origins in New York City to a realm of increasingly bizarre events, ultimately leading to a spiritual awakening fueled by his initial UFO sighting.

For All We Know poses the thought-provoking question: are UFOs tangible manifestations or symbolic representations of realms that transcend our current comprehension? Does the UFO phenomenon serve as a mirror, forcing us to confront our own expectations and revealing a deeper, underlying force at play? This narrative delves into these inquiries, suggesting that the realm of ufology may hold the key to unraveling the true nature of sentient existence. Perhaps hidden behind the veil of the paranormal lies the wellspring of profound wisdom—a domain waiting to be explored. This pursuit is not solely driven by curiosity but also rooted in the pursuit of genuine scientific inquiry.

Only recently, I discovered the work of writers like Dr. Jeffrey Kripal, Dr. Diana Pasulka, Jacques Vallée, Alan Steinfeld, Whitley Streiber, Joshua Cutchin, Mike Clelland, and numerous others who have expanded their understanding of ufology and its intricate connections to the paranormal and spirituality. *For All We Know* proposes the notion that encounters with UFOs bear striking resemblances to spiritual experiences, whether it be through the transcendence achieved by potent music, the sacred ambiance of a church or a humble living room, or the revelation of nature's splendor within a forest. These intensely transformative encounters, including confronting mortality at gunpoint or enduring a loved one passing into the great unknown, alter the trajectory of a person's life.

Through storytelling and narrative, *For All We Know* weaves together multiple subjects: philosophy of mind, cosmology, parapsychology, psychedelics, ufology and more. The reader is invited to embark on a profound journey alongside Matteo, as he gradually unravels the cosmic mysteries hidden within both the mundane and the sublime. I hope that readers will be entertained and inspired by Matteo's spiritual odyssey, and perhaps even discover shared questions, if not shared experiences, along the way.

When I had journeyed half of our life's way
I found myself within a shadowed forest,
for I had lost the path that does not stray.
Ah, it is hard to speak of what it was,
that savage forest, dense and difficult,
which even in recall renews my fear:
so bitter—death is hardly more severe!
But to retell the good discovered there,
I'll also tell of the other things I saw.
—Dante, *Inferno,* Canto I

Foreword

The earliest memory I have is of a UFO. I must have been between two and three years old. It was one of those endless, carefree, gloriously sunny days that only exist as memories in the minds of adults—our very own long Edwardian summers. I aimlessly stood by a gnarly wooden bench in the garden of a house I was only fleetingly aware of as my home, clasping a drink of orange juice. I was alone, as far as I knew.

An unfamiliar humming suddenly punctured my awareness, and a strange object came speeding into view, purposefully circling down from seemingly miles away to just several feet above my head. Then it abruptly stopped. I unthinkingly put my cup of juice down on the bench. Mesmerized by the object, the sunny day momentarily receded, and I found myself seemingly hovering up to meet it, and then in a blink it was gone.

I might never have remembered this encounter if it wasn't for the fact that when I reached back for my drink, and looked into the cup, I saw the object buzzing frantically. Gold and black stripes blurred as it flailed unhappily in the liquid, and I screamed instinctively, empathetically, deep from my core, tossing the cup up into the air in fear. And at the same time, the intensity of the experience, the brief tidal wave of emotion, etched those moments into my mind.

The English opium-eater Thomas de Quincey described the human mind as a palimpsest, with layers of experience imprinted as fading memories on a reused parchment. Looking back on that experience now, I know two things I didn't know then.

Prosaically, I now know that it was a gorgeous bumblebee, or dumbledore as Robert Southey said of that good-natured insect. But moreover, I know that for my past self, whoever that was, it was an unidentified flying object. It was a confrontation with the unknown.

My second oldest memory is of a liminal state—watching my mother hoover that same house, emptied of its contents, before moving to what I always felt was my childhood home. For a long time, I thought that memory to be mundane, a mere fleeting snapshot of the senses, but it marked a childhood transition—the moment I passed through an awareness of my place in the world. These memories underscore the palimpsest because the bursting into life of consciousness is anything but mundane, it is exceptional.

As a writer, memories are the source materials for the fiction of everyday life. I was gently and beautifully reminded of this by reading Mike Fiorito's episodic *For All We Know*—a memorial fiction of the extraordinary, the otherworldly, the transitional. And those ecstatic moments when we each stand out from ourselves, in encounters with UFOs or psychedelics or alike, are always ultimately grounded in the everyday. Memories are interruptions of that foundation, and Mike's writing thoughtfully yields their mysterious secrets.

Robert Dickins
June 2023, London

Borrowing Time

I've always believed in UFOs.

It's 1976. At ten years old, I steal books about spaceships from the library for my bookshelf. I thumb through the pages and stare at the pictures in my bed at night. I want to swim in an ocean of books. Volumes of spaceships and futurology.

I notice something new installed at the entrance to the library near the Ravenswood Projects where I live. It looks like a subway turnstile. I'm suspicious that it's some kind of security system. I grab a few books on spaceships and space travel and hand them to my unwitting friend, Joe.

"Take these and meet me outside," I say.

Whereas I'm a little pip-squeak, Joe is taller and wider. At eleven, he's already starting to show the beginnings of a beard. Wanting to be helpful, Joe grabs the books, putting them in his backpack. As soon as he tries to exit, a detector goes off. *Beep beep beep.* My theory is right: the machines were put there to stop people from stealing books. I'll have to devise another way of obtaining books for my expanding collection. Outside, I apologize to Joe. He's still not sure exactly what happened.

At twelve, in middle school, I continue to be obsessed with spaceships and UFOs. I know I'm onto something. As I lie in bed, thumbing through *Fate*, a UFO magazine I buy weekly, my father passes my doorway and says, "At least read those *Omni* magazines I bought you." *Omni* is a magazine of science fiction and fact. It publishes stories by the preeminent sci-fi writers of the day—Philip K. Dick, Isaac Asimov, Ray Bradbury, Roger

Zelensky, Ursula Le Guin. But it also has articles on new technologies and current science. Aside from being published by Bob Guccione, the same guy who publishes *Penthouse*, it's a respectable journal. I read it cover to cover. Unlike *Omni*, *Fate* publishes articles on psychic abilities, ghosts and hauntings, precognitive dreams, telepathy, and other paranormal topics. I especially love the personal accounts. Why do so many people have these kinds of experiences? How could these accounts be fake?

"Did you hear me?" my father says, louder. My father's voice is deep; it ricochets off the hallway walls. But I don't respond. He's teasing me and I won't let him have the satisfaction.

My mother, Cookie, doesn't have to say anything. Her eyes often lock with mine in silence and hold me in shame.

Although they don't say it aloud, the truth is, I think my parents are worried about my soul. Is this obsession with other worlds some kind of Satanic thing? Can this make me a bad Catholic?

Unlike my brother Paolo, a model student, athlete, and president of his class, I want to escape the world of ambitions. They don't concern me. I'd rather read books on mythology and science fiction and play music with my best friend, Squid. We form a rock group called Gemini (we're both Geminis). He's the drummer, I'm the guitar player and vocalist. Like our heroes Cream, Hendrix, and Led Zeppelin, we play long jams. Sometimes we are pretty good.

Seasons That Pass You By

Two years later, Squid and I start smoking pot. Our music listening becomes deeper. We don't yet realize how perceptive we are, that we are rejecting the bullshit world of the status quo. That we are consciousness pioneers.

Now fourteen, Squid and I pass a joint back and forth in Squid's bedroom, gazing out the window. We're recovering from a traumatic event: I've just had a gun put up to my head. We live in a tough neighborhood.

Being on the sixth floor, it's like we're on top of the Earth. From Squid's window we see the distant rooftops of other project buildings. At this moment, it seems as if our project complex is a chunk of Earth floating out in space, surrounded by a million years. The trees have a bright green shimmer as they sway in the gentle summer breeze.

We're listening to Yes's *Close to the Edge*, one of the many albums lined up on the shelf near the window where the record player sits. The title song blares out of the speakers. Squid's brothers listen to music at full volume, so this isn't unusual in his house. My father would probably call the police on us if I played music this loud.

Close to the Edge opens with the sounds of birds twittering. The music conjures up a distant world: we're on another planet, sitting in a valley between mountains, spaceships flying overhead. In the sky on this planet there are two suns and a gigantic purple-red moon, visible during the day. Suddenly the band's music blasts from the speakers, like a titanic UFO is crash-landing on

9

our project building. The room shakes as the music screams out of the walls.

"Yes is my favorite band," shouts Squid over the music.

"They're my favorite band with Bill Bruford as drummer," I say, leaning into his ear to be heard. It never occurs to us that we can lower the music.

"I know, I know. You like Bruford."

Squid likes the Yes configuration with Alan White on drums. I like Bill Bruford. Bruford is more of a jazz drummer, he plays offbeat rhythms—wonderfully unpredictable. White is more of a straight-ahead rock drummer. Squid likes the live Yes albums, and I prefer the studio albums.

Squid and I have this discussion for hours while smoking weed. We talk about the worlds that Yes weaves with their music. Worlds of bucolic beauty. Mountain landscapes floating in space. Visions of a future in which humans have become spiritually and socially advanced. But Squid and I don't use words like bucolic. We don't know those words, though Squid writes reams of poetry that he sometimes shows me. But we're drawn to the poetic lyrics in Yes's songs. And we're fascinated by the interesting sounds of the instruments: mandolins, church organs, harpsichords, pedal-steel, nylon- and twelve-string guitars. There are also a lot of futuristic sounds in Yes's music: Moog synthesizers, Mellotrons and Hammond organs. The mix of ancient and futuristic makes Yes's music sound timeless. That, along with the legato singing and polyphonic harmonies, make it seem as thought their vocals are sung by all the angels and saints in heaven.

We may not know what we're doing, but we know in our bones that we're connected to the most important journey of a human soul. That music can transport you. Deliver you. That music is a form of time travel.

Squid's mother bangs on the bedroom wall, shouting over the music, asking us to lower the volume. She must have been banging for a while. Squid turns down the knob on the stereo.

"Thank you," we hear from the hallway. She doesn't sound angry; she practically sings her thank you. The music must have been at rock-concert levels.

"I can't believe what happened last night," says Squid in a hushed voice.

"I know, I totally freaked out."

"Why didn't you hand him your radio?"

This is not an easy question to answer. Sure, I panicked, the black-metal gun to my head made me go blank. But there was much more to it than that. I had begged my dad for months to get me the radio. It's a Panasonic with a cassette player. I saved up for months to get it; he gave me half. Then he insisted I keep it at home so it wouldn't get stolen. But this little plastic box with knobs brings voices from another dimension. It tunes into frequencies on the electromagnetic spectrum that only initiated beings can hear. Beings from anywhere in the universe. It can communicate in two ways. They can hear us, and we can hear them. Who are they? I don't know now and I didn't know back then.

"I mean, just running away like that from the kid with the gun, that was crazy," says Squid, lighting up the joint again. The song's chorus rings out over the speakers. I know Squid knows what I'm thinking. Despite the events of last night, the music calls to us. We're just kids, unable to explain that the music transports us to a safer, more beautiful place. A place less dangerous than the projects. Not as filthy. No dead steel factories or abandoned buildings in this world. In Yes's music we journey to places with mountains, rainbows, and rivers. Some of these places are right here in front of us. Sometimes, they are scattered across the galaxies.

"This might be my all-time favorite album," Squid finally says.

"Even with Bruford on drums?"

"Maybe," he draws out slowly. He's patting his head with his fingers. "I might put *Yessongs* on the same level with *Close to the Edge*."

I nod along with him, pleased.

"Do you think that guy would have shot me?" I ask.

"What?" Squid replies. He always says *what* when he's not sure. There is nothing bitter or mean in Squid. He loves the crazy shit I do, but he wouldn't be the person to do that crazy thing. And he doesn't want to upset me.

"Do you think that guy would have shot me?"

"But he didn't shoot you."

"He put the gun up to my head."

"But he didn't pull the trigger." Squid smiles. "Maybe because he knew you were a sick motherfucker."

"But he was one click away."

"He was." Nodding, he adds, "It would have been over in one second."

It's Squid's quick answer that gets to me. I picture how my body would have looked, splayed on the concrete, a puddle of thick red blood gushing from my head like gas from a busted fuel tank. I shiver for a second, but Squid doesn't notice.

"But you, you were a madman, running away like that. I mean, the guy would have shot you if you simply flinched." He waits a few beats. "You must have known that, right?"

I don't have an answer for him.

The joint between my index finger and thumb has gone out.

I light it up again. Squid adds, "I'm just glad you're here and we can listen to music together. No one else hears music like we do."

I'm choked up by his words. We both know how close that call was. Close to the edge. I take a pull on the joint and pass it back to him. We try to avoid looking at each other's watery eyes.

Then Squid reaches over to make the music louder as the final chorus plays on the stereo. The refrain on the title song *Close to the Edge* reminds me of how I traversed the border of life and death, at one instant being both dead and alive. I hear the ghost echo of a gunshot in my brain. In that moment, my blood feels cold and still.

Pretending to be a Star

My father tries to encourage my interest in "outer space," thinking it will make me more scientific, even a better student. He buys me sci-fi magazines and books. After he buys Carl Sagan's book *Cosmos* for me, we watch the television series together on Saturday mornings. This kind of thing will get me out of the project neighborhood we live in. My father is well- intentioned.

"You like this, right?" Dad asks.

"I really love the stuff about SETI," I say.

"Search for Extraterrestrial Intelligence?"

"I love the Golden Record that was placed inside the Voyager to convey who we are to other intelligent beings," I add.

"There's a lot of practical science in the program, too. Formation of planets, of stars. Black holes. And Sagan is a wonderful narrator."

"I'm interested in what else is out there."

"We may never know."

"We won't know if we don't explore. What could be more incredible than to encounter another species?"

Dad and I often have this back and forth. My brother Paolo and sister Patty never have this kind of debate with him.

"In the meantime, science is helpful in a million ways," says my father. "Medical technology, computers, and things like that."

I know my father's agenda. I don't want to give my dad what he wants to hear. I want to say what I want to say. I just can't believe we're the only thinking species in this universe. That's the only thing I think or care about. And my father knows it.

One cold winter night in January, bored and restless, I tell my mother and father that I'm going to Squid's and Squid tells his mother that he's coming to my apartment.

"I'm going to Squid's," I say as I rush out of the apartment, impressed at how smart our plan is. From Squid's roof, I shout into the wind, hoping my voice will reach his window one floor below.

"Squid, can you hear me?"

"Yes," he answers. We can't see each other.

"I'm ready," I say.

Leaning over the thin wire fence that borders the roof, I reach out for the jacket Squid is flinging up to me. The key is to snatch them as he throws them upward. As my hands search the night air, it doesn't occur to me that I might fall off the roof. I'm sure it doesn't occur to Squid either.

"I got it," I say, grabbing hold of Squid's jacket. Time for my coat. We meet in the sixth-floor stairwell. Before we head out for a walk, Squid suggests going back on the roof to smoke a cigarette. Across the river the buildings of the Manhattan skyline sparkle like burning amethysts.

"People would pay big money to get this view of the city," says Squid, taking a drag on a cigarette.

"We're just lucky," I say. It doesn't occur to us that we live in a project tenement. That everyone who lives here would rather live somewhere else.

But the view is undeniable. It is like being on an asteroid floating above the city. And even though this is a project tenement, the skyline suggests infinite possibilities. It's all happening over there, across the East River. In more ways than one, that world, the world of Manhattan, is far away from us. But the bejeweled buildings stand majestically before us as if they are there for us. For only us. Despite the filth in our building, the pee on the floor (which is sometimes mine), the graffiti on the walls (sometimes mine), and the stench from the Department of Sanitation depot across the street, we're granted a glimpse of paradise with that skyline. Especially on a cold night like this. The air is fresh on my face. The heat from the cigarette feels good. I take another long drag and sweep my head from left to right, scooping up the view. Starting on the far left is the Brooklyn Bridge, next is the Twin Towers. Going north, I stop at the Empire State Building, then the Chrysler Building. North to the Citibank Building on 54th Street. Just east of the Citibank Building is the Queensborough Bridge linking Manhattan to Queens. Turning my head further north, I see the Triborough Bridge, which connects Queens, Manhattan, and the Bronx.

"What's that? asks Squid.

I shake my head, not knowing what he's talking about. For some reason the taste of burning sulfur is on my lips.

"That little moving light over there. Find the needle on the Empire State Building, now move over about an index finger. Look just above that."

I see something. It's moving. A bright bluish spherical object.

"It looks like an airplane."

"Airplanes don't fly that low over Manhattan."

"Maybe it just looks that way."

Suddenly, the sphere moves in a direct line to a distant part of the night sky. Then it zips back. For a moment it returns, shining as if on fire. The whole sky lights up. A great wind whooshes past me. Then the light dims and shrinks, bolting deep into the dark of the night, as if pretending to be a star.

"Did you see that?" I ask Squid.

"I saw it. That shit was weird."

"Do you think it's what I think it is?"

"A UFO?"

"That's what I think."

"What should we do?" asks Squid.

"I don't know. I'm not even sure what just happened."

Church as a UFO

Because Long Island City High School, which is only a few blocks away from our apartment building, has a reputation for drop-outs and drug users, my parents insist that I go to Monsignor McClancy High School, an all-boys Catholic institution. Also, my parents are concerned about my pot smoking and what they consider to be wild behavior.

I don't ever talk about it, admit it to anyone, or even consciously know it, but I love being in McClancy's church. Even though I horse around with friends in the pews, I also look up at the vaulted ceilings and meditate on the stained-glass windows. I especially love the stations of the cross. I now realize that the stations are very similar to the arc of Jung's individuation: Jesus is condemned to death, struggles with carrying the cross, he is stripped, nailed to the cross, dies on the cross, laid to be buried in a tomb—and we know that he will rise again. As the light streams through the stained-glass windows, I pause on each portrait. They show compassion and love. Jesus allows his prisoners to beat and abuse him, knowing that he will be nailed to the cross to die. He is comforted by others along the way.

With one eye on the imagery in the church, I show Mickey Ness the joint I rolled in class earlier that day. I'm having two communications at once: Mickey and the portraits. I'm deeply moved by their portrayals of compassion. Yes, those fuckers are going to kill Jesus and enjoy it. But others feel Jesus's pain and suffering. And that's what this is all about. Offering examples of kindness in a world of cruelty. The colors on the stained-glass portraits are made brighter by the light shining through them. I'm in a spangled dome. My eyes explode with colors.

The church organ pipes let out a blast. Mickey Ness cups his hand near my ear to talk. I tell him I can't hear him and point to Brother Craig, who's looking over at us. *Tell me later.* I'm trying to shut him up. *Listen to the music,* I'm thinking. Now the voices from the choir join in with the organ. Both the organ and the choir are on the second level above us. We can hardly see them, as if they are angels singing down from heaven. I am lost in the hush of silence and rainbow images and find myself dreaming.

Maybe it's the pot from last night, but I see the church as a kind of spaceship now. The music, the stained-glass windows, the cross-like structure of the church, from the narthex to the apse, and the gigantic statue of Christ nailed to the cross—all of this launches me into another world. I am flying. Journeying across time and space.

Mickey Ness motions for me to engage with his joking. I gesture towards Brother Craig as if to say, *Stop it already, we'll get in trouble,* though it must seem arbitrary. I've clowned around in these moments dozens of times before.

But at this moment, I'm quiet inside. My breath stills. Oceanic sounds and feelings wash over me. From my toes to the crown of my head, I'm an illumination, bathed in pure light. Glowing. On fire. The church trembles like a nuclear reactor, as if it's about to burn a hole in the fabric of space and time, plunging me into another world. I'm ready. I hope, as I break the skin of space-time, angels capture and escort me. To a world of towering marble buildings speckled with gold, where super beings fly unhinged from gravity and there is no separation of mind from cosmos. Where cosmos *is* mind.

"Hey Matteo," says Mickey Ness, "you coming?" Mass is

over. I'm still standing in the pew, my hands held together in prayer.

"You getting churchy on us?" asks Micky Ness.

"No, man" I say. "Fuck you, I fell asleep."

Andromeda Lounge

I'm not a heavy metal fan. But Joe insists we see King Diamond.
It is 1980.

"This is great music, man," he says. "They're amazing musicians. It's not just guitar shredding."

"What's the band's name again?" asks Squid.

"King Diamond," replies Joe with a straight face.

Squid and I laugh.

"Trust me," pleads Joe, shaking his head to underscore the seriousness of the band and his opinion of them.

But Squid and I are doubtful. Our love of heavy metal music stops at Black Sabbath and Deep Purple. Joe is deep into groups like Megadeth, Iron Maiden and Motorhead. He has the albums, wears their T-shirts. Squid and I are more into progressive and psychedelic rock, not just Yes but Jethro Tull and King Crimson. Psychedelic groups write songs about other worlds, about the love of the universe, of knowledge. That kind of crap. They transport us out of drab Long Island City with its factories and project buildings sending us in fantastic new realms. The album covers are fairytale-like. A chunk of earth floating out into space. Extraterrestrial creatures. And the instruments they play—and play well. Mandolins, acoustic guitars. Moog synthesizers. Spacey far out shit. Somewhere between *Lord of the Rings* and *Star Trek*. This is where we want to be. Lost in the cosmic swirl. Not stuck in the dismal shithole of the projects or the satanic hellhole of heavy metal.

Joe persists. He begs. Let's face it, he doesn't want to go

alone—all the way to L'Amour in Bay Ridge, Brooklyn, from Queens. And he wants us to like his music, too.

We take the train to 62nd Street in Brooklyn. To make the long train ride bearable, Squid and I smoke a joint in between the train cars. We hold onto the train handles, passing a joint with our free hand, swaying with the stopping and starting of the train. The great thing about riding between train cars is that you can do anything. You can smoke cigarettes, pee on the tracks, or vomit into the rushing air if you must. This is the NYC subway system in 1980. There are no rules. It is a lawless land.

Before we head back into the train car, Squid and I each pop a hit of mescaline. Joe never takes drugs. He just watches us as we slowly devolve into idiots.

Sitting in the train car, we laugh and joke. The train moves slowly, creaking its way to Brooklyn. There is garbage swirling around the train cars and graffiti on its walls. As littered and filthy as the train car looks, it begins to glow and shimmer.

By the time we get to our stop, the mescaline and weed have fully kicked in. Walking down the street the neon signs speak to me in some secret electronic language, luring me into the stores over which they hang. Maybe aliens hide behind the counters in the stores.

From the outside, L'Amour looks like a humdrum bar, but when the door swings open, the bright velvet curtains and ornate chandeliers give the impression we've stepped into a medieval dungeon. The mescaline is now fully pumping through my brain. Colors are sharper, sounds more articulated. I hear wind in the drum cymbals and radar signals in the guitar notes.

There are at least three floors inside the club and little alcoves with couches where you can make out or smoke weed in a more private place. Since the band hasn't yet started, we wander around the club exploring its hidden chambers.

The castle-like atmosphere is enhanced by the chalky white-faced zombie fans who sashay through the venue. The dead look in their eyes is a little ominous. Along with the thundering guitar sounds and heavy bass riffs pounding the walls, it feels like we are being led into a slaughterhouse. Machines blow curls of smoke that twirl and twist in the arena lights, taking on the changing colors. Lights flash and blink to the music. The only things missing are lightning and rain.

Style-wise, Joe, Squid and I are completely out of place here. We wear simple dungaree pants and T-shirts. We don't have gothic outfits, make-up, or long purple fingernails. And our hair is short and coily, not straight and long.

Suddenly all attention turns toward center stage. It becomes dark and silent. The zombies gather around us; I wonder if they will try to eat us in a savage frenzy.

Then the lights flood the stage. The band, materializing out of nowhere, begins playing. The music sounds like the groan of an enormous metallic whale chained to a cage in Hell.

As the thick smoke from the stage clears, a studded coffin emerges from the blackness. I hear grunting from the zombies around me. Are they alive, or are they dead already? Mouths open, hands extended, they eagerly await the moment their leader will tear into them like a devil, ripping open their stomachs with his fangs and claws.

Joe frantically points to the stage. He's whispering to me and Squid, but we can't hear him. We want to laugh but between the mescaline and the weed, we are scared out of our wits. I swear I see bats flying around us. This is getting serious now. And then, the coffin slowly opens. The leader of the dead zombies, King Diamond, steps out. He sticks his tongue out and makes threatening faces, opening his mouth wide, pushing his eyeballs out of his head.

As soon as he starts singing, the zombies begin shaking their heads in unison with the thudding rhythms, as if their long hair is clapping to the music. Shaking their skulls turning their brains to pulp.

We stand in awe, hands by our sides, hearts beating rapidly.

Singing into a microphone shaped like a human skull, King Diamond's face is painted with blood, as if his zombie worshippers had chewed into his cheeks. At some point, King Diamond spins and whirls to the music, the stage a vortex where demonic wizards and spirits swim in an embryonic cell. Their bodies liquefy and ooze in the placental walls, their essences melting to the hypnotic rhythms and screaming guitar frequencies. This is way beyond just music. This is a consecrated transfiguration. We are witnessing the beating heart of the universe, everything that has ever lived and died. All existences metamorphosing into a single blood cell that pulses and pumps. It is nothing short of a possession.

Goblins and demons follow us home, some of them disguised as ordinary subway passengers. We move to different cars to escape them and because we can't stop laughing. Every time we do stop laughing, we get serious, concerned that some evil spirit will attack us with spikes and toss our severed limbs to other flesh-eating fiends. We aren't sure if the train is going down into Hell or just west and north back to Queens.

Somehow, we make it home, stumbling back to the Ravenswood project building where we live at almost four in the morning. A pink silver streaks the sky, suggesting that the world will be once again be wrested from the demons.

Tom Turkey's Tie-Dye

Tom Turkey wears a tie-dyed shirt and loose-fitting yoga pants; his long blond hair hanging in dreadlocks down his back. He is tanned, like he spent the summer trekking through the Mexican Baja, meditating with shamans.

My friend Ivan and I sit on a bench in the Ravenswood Projects smoking weed with Tom Turkey and Dakota, his girlfriend. Dakota thumbs a paperback copy of *Leaves of Grass*, reading passages aloud. Bright green leaves bedeck the cover of the book.

"Keep your face always toward the sunshine and shadows will fall behind you," says Dakota, reciting Whitman with a slight lisp, slowly enunciating each word.

Dakota sits cross-legged on the bench with *Leaves* perched in her hand. Despite her hippie dress, her long thin legs manage to escape into view. As I listen to her words, I am thinking about how smooth and perfect her legs are. Her skin is like the white contours of bleached sand dunes. Dakota doesn't wear any makeup, yet her perfect lips glisten a light pink hue.

"Hey man," says Tom Turkey to Ivan and me, stroking the braids of his long hair, "I got Suns and I'll give them to you for three dollars apiece, but each of you have to take six hits now."

Ivan's been talking about taking acid all summer.

Neither Ivan nor I respond to Turkey's dare.

Turning away from us, Turkey removes a dulcimer from the case slung over his shoulder. The dulcimer is carved with miniature runes and faces of wood nymphs. He strums, plucking

Lord-of-the-Rings-like melodies, pausing to school us about the LSD.

"I risk a lot transporting this back from California," he says, then continues strumming. "It's too good to sell to just anyone. I don't want to waste these on amateurs."

Turkey puts down the dulcimer to light a bowl of weed. The bowl, too, is decorated with runes, maybe the dulcimer and bowl came as a set. Dragging on the bowl like he's sucking air from a hole in the ground to survive, he lets out a massive plume. I imagine him exhaling smoke into tree-nymph and fairy shapes, like Gandalf did in *Lord of the Rings*.

"Of course, if you don't want them..." says Turkey, his voice trailing off. He hands the bowl to Ivan. Ivan has a big, crooked nose, bad teeth, and long scraggly hair. Whereas Turkey is suave and handsome in his hippie-dippy outfit, Ivan looks like Magwitch from *Great Expectations*. We call Ivan "Spare Parts" because he looks like he was assembled from discarded parts in a machine shop. One arm is jammed in the socket; the other arm shorter and slightly curved at the elbow. Buck teeth hammered into his gums like tombstones.

Emerging from his wordless chrysalis, Ivan looks up, finally, saying "we'll take them," inhaling smoke from the bowl. As he coughs, he nods at me for agreement. "These are the Suns I've been telling you about," says Ivan. "This isn't like the shitty acid you get in Washington Square Park. This is Owsley acid," he says, like he knows.

That summer I'd read *Doors of Perception* and *The Electric Kool-Aid Acid Test*, preparing for an epic psychedelic trip. I had even taken half a tab of blotter acid a few weeks ago. But six hits? Ivan said that he'd felt the beating-heart center of Cygnus X-1 tripping on six hits of acid. He also told me he took acid every day a few years ago but then had to stop. "I started to get creepy, started losing my mind." And I can't imagine him any more insane than he already is.

As I sit there on the park bench, swinging my feet back and forth, I think of what's ahead of me. Next fall I'll attend college. Taking acid is my pre-college workshop, like summer school with Timothy Leary.

"I'll do it, too," I say to Turkey.

Turkey hands us the Sun hits and we give him our money. We immediately take the acid, letting the paper melt on our tongues. It's tasteless.

In the shade of the trees, the light summer breeze sprays a soft tapping of kisses on my face. We are all stoned now from the weed. Turkey again starts plucking his dulcimer as Dakota sings in a high-pitched voice, accompanying him. The words of the song describe ancient humans taking hallucinogens. The world was in order and perfect at that time, the song suggests. Believing all this crap, I'm getting tingles down my spine. Their voices sound pretty good together. I'm quietly wondering why we can't go back to being perfect storybook creatures, achieving cosmic balance and harmony with the universe.

When they stop playing, Turkey reminds us that he's the grandchild of Aldous Huxley.

He's said this shit before.

"My father moved from England in the 50s to get away from the Huxley name," Turkey says.

"Grandpa Aldous used to read *The Tibetan Book of the Dead* to me when I was a baby, my mother says."

I don't believe Turkey, but I'm stoned and want to believe him. I imagine him in a baby jinnee outfit as Grandpa Aldous rocks him to sleep.

The truth of the matter is that I'm jealous of Turkey. I'd like to travel the world with a beautiful woman, searching for shamans and wisdom teachers. Instead, the closest I have to a wisdom teacher is my slightly deformed and satanic friend, Ivan.

As the acid courses through my bloodstream, I see a light dalliance of colors shining off the trees, the bench and swelling up from the ground. I start playing with the antenna on a radio I hadn't noticed. It has been silent the whole time, as if spying on us. As the antenna flickers back and forth, it splashes a spectrum of rainbow colors.

"I can see the waves," I say aloud. Ivan laughs.

Now that the acid is taking effect, Turkey gets restless. He didn't want to hang out with amateurs; he just wanted to make sure that we had taken the acid. For a goof.

As I turn to look at Turkey, I am transfixed by Dakota's dress. I can't see her long sexy legs anymore. Her dress is roaring with color, rippling like a Mexican sunset, streaks of yellow engulfing streaks of pink.

Acid makes me think out loud for some reason. I describe my hallucinations.

"This is like the River Styx," I say, pointing at a long rivulet of color, imagining my pupils as big and wet as giant goldfish. "This purple band is gurgling lava."

Dakota laughs at me. I'm completely serious. I want to impress her. Maybe Turkey recites *The Tibetan Book of the Dead* to her. He speaks like a T.S. Eliot poem. I'm sure Turkey is wise when he tells her about his cosmic visions. I'm sure she sees me the way I see Ivan, an ugly moron.

"We have to get going," says Tom Turkey.

I don't want Dakota to leave, whether she likes me or feels sorry for me. And I am convinced she'll make sure my trip goes well. Being left alone with Ivan could turn out badly.

"Happy trails," says Turkey, "wherever your airplane happens to land." At that moment, I hate Turkey. How could she go out with him? Doesn't she realize he's a fucking phony? That bullshit about being Huxley's grandson.

Turkey takes Dakota by the hand and slings the dulcimer case over his shoulder, like he's galloping off into the sunset. Seeing the sadness in my eyes, Dakota takes a step towards me and leans over to give me a kiss and muss my hair. Her lips touch my cheek. Even though her kiss is like a big sister's, the sensation sends rushes across my body, like I've been touched by lightning.

The kiss ricochets across nerve endings, rumbles in my guts and prickles my scalp, exploding finally in my fingertips and toes. I snap out of my daydream.

"How will the airplane take you home?" I ask. I didn't mean to say that. Dakota and Turkey giggle.

Walking away, Dakota waves goodbye. Even down the block she is still waving. It's like a game we're playing. I keep waving until she is the size of a baseball. Then only a wavy line. Even when she disappears, I see her as a swirl of pink in the distance. I don't know how long this game has gone on for. I start to cry. I'll never meet a woman like her. Tears pour down my face like runoff from a river. I turn away, wiping them off. I look to see if Ivan notices. He doesn't.

Ivan and I are alone.

The acid shoots through my veins. The ground sparkles with a rainbow shimmer. Even the little rocks on the ground are speckled with diamonds. The leaves on the trees are so bright they look like they will explode into a million tiny pieces. I see visual memes of the *Leaves of Grass* book cover everywhere: on the trees, on the ground, in the sky.

"Let's go to Roosevelt Island," says Ivan. Roosevelt Island has parks and trees. The East River flows between it and Manhattan. I signal agreement, my head bobbing back and forth, a wooden puppet incapable of using words.

We walk down to Rainey Park, then onto the bridge that takes us to Roosevelt Island. I hallucinate visions of stories being told on the surface of the water far below us, a continuation of the mythic tales that Turkey and Dakota had talked about. I wish Dakota was walking hand in hand with me.

The face of Poseidon forms on the water and speaks. I ask Ivan if he can also see Poseidon.

"Yes, I see him," he says. "He wants to eat your brains." That's not what I want to hear.

"Fuck you, you're just making that shit up," I say. Ivan cracks a sinister smile. With his long scraggly hair combed over one side of his head, he looks like a fugitive from the Manson family.

Soon my stomach feels nauseous. My insides swish around like I've swallowed a snake.

The sun's rays pound down on us. I am sweating profusely. Each pump of fresh blood through my heart is a dizzying rush of acid.

Six hits? And from Turkey? I should have known better.

"You know Poseidon is a minion of Satan," says Ivan, contorting his face, his eyes red.

"I'm not feeling so well so shut the fuck up, man," I say. "I think the acid was too strong."

We keep walking, but I have to stop. I sit on a bench, hyperventilating.

"Let's go home," I say.

"You can never go home."

"Either we go home," I say, "or I'm going to the emergency

room."

My body begins shutting down, the acid arresting my senses. The sun is too big for me; it's everywhere in the sky. Like an egg leaking its yolk, the sun's heat is dripping on me, heavy, syrupy. I hold my chest, breathing heavily.

Seeing me squirm on the bench, Ivan finally agrees to go home.

My head an overflowing fishbowl, I see monsters peering out of pits of hell. I put my hands over my face to hide the demon faces, but they emerge from the darkness of my hands. Dogs hanging from lampposts. Charred bodies of eyeless children. Grinning devils, their eye sockets running with blood, spiders pouring from their apertures.

"We're almost home," says Ivan, knowing that I'm in bad shape. "Don't worry, you'll be fine." Even though he's an asshole he knows I could fall off the face of the earth without his help. And he'd have to answer to someone for it. The cops, my parents. Who knows?

When we finally get to his house, I am relieved to be out of the sun. We couldn't have gone to my house. I look haunted, like a zombie, pale and frightened. My parents would have called a doctor. Or an exorcist.

Now in his bedroom, Ivan puts on music. He leaves me alone and as I lie on his bed; an upside-down volcano erupts from the ceiling.

Ivan returns with a pitcher full of red Kool-Aid. The color and consistency of the liquid are soothing. I drink the Kool-Aid in long gulps. Drinking a river of easygoing forever redness soothes my brain. The dimness of the room feels good. The sun seeps in from the cracks in the shades, instead of blaring down on us like an angry god.

My central nervous system slows from the express train to hell; I'm back on the local. The walls heave and shrink, but gracefully, a gigantic cinematic screen playing the history of the universe before my eyes. But it's not just visual, it's emotional. I cry for the birth of our sun and the formation of the galaxies. I feel sad that my parents still live in the Ravenswood Projects.

"See," Ivan says.

"See what?"

"See how cool it is."

"Yeah, it's cool."

"But you wigged out, man."

"It was all your fault," I say. "You're a fucking maniac. What's with all the Satan talk?"

"I like being in the belly of the beast," he says. "You don't learn anything from the good trips."

"Well, I don't need to learn anything. Leave me alone with that shit."

As I take another slug of the Kool-Aid, the music smoothly races around my brain. My thoughts are like hamsters on a wheel.

"This is here all of the time," says Ivan. "We just can't see it. But the ancients could see this shit," he says passing me a joint.

This is, like, how the Mayans lived, I think to myself. The Mayans took hallucinogens, looked up into the skies and saw into the future. These trips bridge you to another reality, another time and place, like Turkey said. All you need do is take these little pieces of paper and you're projected into another realm.

"The music holds the secrets too," I say, philosophizing and talking shit. "It's like everyone who takes this shit can read the messages in the music." Everywhere is a portal to another world.

"We can do this again," says Ivan.

"No fucking talk about demons."

"Okay, no demons next time. But you're missing out man."

"Don't be a fucking asshole, okay?"

As I sit across from this unhinged mutant, no longer beating back a sea of demons, I know that I have peered outside of the little world that has previously bound my experience.

As fucked up as Ivan is, he has opened a door. Having gone first to hell, my mind is leaning into the sunshine. Beyond our glorious sun, I see the spirals of the Milky Way. And this is only the beginning. The universe is boundless. I'll go wherever my airplane takes me.

An Ebbing Red Sea

Ivan and I take LSD again the following week.

About an hour later, listening to Lothar and the Hand People, I observe the ceiling in Ivan's bedroom melting in slow motion. "Lothar" is like the soundtrack to a horror film. Ivan insists on listening to deranged music while tripping on acid.

I walk out of the bedroom into his mother's living room. Here, in the throne room of Moses, golden paisley couches perch on an ebbing Red Sea.

Ivan follows me into the living room. He pulls his chess set from a shelf, resembling a maniac demon.

I stare down at the chessboard. The squares move around. If I put a piece down, the square changes from black to white, sometimes shading in between. The golden colors of the couch and the brown squares of the chessboard blink in unison like Christmas lights.

Running into the kitchen, Ivan returns to the living room table with a butcher's knife and an orange. Ivan points the knife at me, then begins slicing the orange.

I should leave at this moment.

I look back at him serenely. If he wants to kill me, someone or something will surely save me. I feel invincible. This is what drugs do to you.

I smile.

Ivan smiles back, like a deranged Cheshsire cat.

After cutting the orange open, he begins motioning with the knife, pointing at my finger.

I hold my hand out to challenge him, as if to say, *Here, cut my finger off if you have the guts.*

We look into the well of each other's eyes.

He slams the knife down on my finger. Blood spurts; a purple blob splotches the corner of his glasses. A rush of pain flushes through my body as if someone had dropped an entire building on my finger. The fucking idiot nearly cut my finger off.

Philosophy Major

When I attend New York University two years later, I live at home and commute to the Village. At twenty, studying Kierkegaard and reading Hemingway, I come home at the end of the day to my father asking me how many pork chops I want and lecturing me on Jimmy Roselli.

"He sings in the real Neapolitan dialect," my father repeats endlessly. *How many times do you need to tell me this?* I think.

The day I tell my mother and father I have declared myself a philosophy major, they are shocked.

"What is this philosophy?" my father asks that night at dinner, making it sound like a sinister political orientation. He isn't ignorant, but he didn't go to college. He hasn't read a philosophy book in his life.

Mom watches me hold my fork. She doesn't look at me; she looks into me. Her gaze is as persistent as the air around me.

When I talked about my decision to declare a philosophy major with Ivan a few weeks before, I was triumphant. Ivan of course supports me, in fact, encourages me. But also, he tried to cut my finger off a few years earlier.

He chokes on the joint he passed me and says it was the smart thing to do.

"Dude man, Harrison Ford was a philosophy major. Alex Trebek, too. Besides, dude," he says, tossing back his long mane of unwashed dirty blonde hair, "like, you're into it, man. You've got to groove with what's happening, man. Dude, like, wherever you are, there you are, you know what I mean? You've got to live out your trip. That's like totally philosophical and shit."

He pauses, releasing a plume of pot smoke.

"I've decided to go to forestry school, dude. I want to be a forest ranger. Get the fuck out of the city, away from the steel and machines, away from this fucking decay and corruption."

He passes me the joint.

"In this life maybe I'll be a ranger. In another life, man, maybe I'll be like a tree or a bird or a fucking rabbit. Or like, maybe I'll be an alien from another galaxy, man. The thing is you must find your path, like Don Juan says, man. Your path is philosophy. You can like totally be a philosopher. Go around the world solving problems, getting cats out of their Babylon mind, man."

His eyes widen.

"Look man, you can become like a resident philosopher to the Rainbow People. You could travel around, live in nature, like be totally naked all the time and get high."

I hand him back the joint thinking, *Yeah, I wouldn't mind being a traveling, naked philosopher, smoking weed and meeting pretty hippie girls.* But I also know that it sounds like bullshit.

As I sit at dinner with my parents, I realize that since they are not stoned, my arguments need to be a little stronger. I wish I could get high with them and discuss my future.

With her typical parental scrutiny, Cookie asks, "What do you study in philosophy?"

"Well, you know, like, you study, like what's the nature of good and bad, what is real—"

She cuts me off with a sharp stare, her brown eyes growing smaller and more suspicious by the second. They blast sulfur and fire, fuming little Sicilian nuclear beetles.

Elbow on the table, her fork in midair, Cookie says, "Do

you mean to tell me you are working your ass off to pay for a private university education so you can learn about reality? Look around you. Look at this," she shouts, pointing to our project apartment.

She should know. Cookie is the rock upon which we all have stood. Her face is dark like the earth itself. She trusts things like the soil, water, and the sound of wind. This business of philosophy is bullshit. It doesn't put food on the table or pay the rent.

"Why don't you do something useful like your brother and sister? Business. Medicine. Do something practical."

"It's what I want to do. Harrison Ford was a philosophy major," I say.

My comment is met with a fierce silence. My father shakes his head. "We want what's best for you. Neither of us went to college; we didn't have the opportunity. But we know how important it is. It's really not a joking matter."

"Look, I have to study something that can sustain my interest for the next few years."

"The accountant at my job studied accounting in college and then took night classes in subjects he was interested in," says Cookie, looking at me like she wants to bounce my head off the table. She will save my life even if she has to kill me.

Trying to find a way out of this my father asks, "What can you do with a philosophy major?"

Sitting up straight, I prepare to take on his question. Here is my opportunity to set the record straight.

"You can do anything with philosophy."

"Which means it prepares you for nothing in particular," says my father.

"Not really. You learn how to write well, how to think and communicate clearly," I say, realizing how I am not demonstrating these skills. I lamely try to defend myself. I wish I could employ the Socratic method on them to make my point, cornering them with clever questions until I force them to agree with me.

In a desperate grasp for something hopeful to say, I repeat what my Philosophy of Mind professor had said earlier in the semester.

"Philosophy majors frequently go into law school. They handed out an article in class last week saying that philosophy majors score highest on the LSAT test."

My mother relaxes her shoulders, loosening the granite look on her face.

"So, you want to be a lawyer?" says Cookie in her Lower East Side accent.

For a moment I am victorious. They are both basking in my glorious future. Out of the projects, law degree in hand. Backyard. Plush carpet, not like the tattered mat in our living room.

I let the moment last.

"Well, ah, not exactly," I say.

They look at each other, then back at me.

"Well, you know, I wouldn't want to represent the law in this country. We live in a diseased society. A society that condones slavery, empire building, environmental destruction, and is indifferent to the life of the soul."

I hate myself for sounding like Ivan.

"Is this what you study in philosophy?" my father asks, as if I've been attending satanic rituals, eating raw animal flesh, and drinking animal blood from a chalice.

"Not exactly. This is just stuff on my mind."

"You've got to grow up, kid. You've got to do something with your life. Believe me; I know how important making money is. I know. You don't want to live like we have. That's what I'm trying to tell you, goddammit."

"You're right. I don't want to live like we have." We live in the projects. Our necks chained to my father's gambling.

"Don't be a smartass. We're trying to help you. Someday you'll understand."

I want to say, *Why did you encourage me to go to school in the first place?* But I just say, "I know, Dad, I know," rolling my eyes, hating them for not understanding the predicament they've put me in.

The Tree as UFO

I've again just bought four tabs of LSD from Tom Turkey for three dollars each. Tom Turkey, the hippie guru who comes around our neighborhood with his girlfriends, showing off his stash of drugs: weed, hash, LSD, and mushrooms. The tabs are tiny squares, smaller than an aspirin, and decorated with rainbow-colored suns.

A few days later, my friend Paul—who is also eighteen—and I take the two hits of the sun acid tabs each when I meet him on the street. We head to Paul's house a few blocks away and up to his room in the attic. His parents are away that Saturday night.

Because Paul's room is in the attic, the ceiling is shaped in the form of a triangle. Like a church spire. There is plush orange and brown carpet on the floor, early 80s style. Around the room are posters of Led Zeppelin, The Who and other rock groups.

As the acid kicks in, we listen to Bill Cosby's *Why Is There Air?* album. Cosby's voice begins to double, triple and quadruple. In a matter of seconds, I can't hear any words, they multiply in a dizzying cascade of ricocheting sounds.

"Can you hear what he's saying?" I ask.

Paul shakes his head no. The speakers are making the sounds more echoey.

We laugh hysterically, looking at Cosby's "I don't know" gesture on the album cover. While I'm laughing my head off, I'm also worried that I'll never be able to understand English again. Have I lost my ability to speak and to understand words?

Maybe thirty minutes later, fully into the acid trip, I marvel at Paul's courage. While I'm freaking out just a little bit, he's completely unafraid, or so it seems. The walls bend and warp in sync with the music. Pockets in Paul's bedroom wall reveal portals to other universes. I spot little dots where time stands still. Other apertures show how the stars were formed. I feel some other intelligence talking directly to my heart. There are no words said.

Playing on Paul's stereo is "Outside My Window" by Cream. The song sounds like it's pouring out of the walls, as if the music is now a river that we're floating down. There are wondrous worlds behind every rock and stone at the bottom of this river.

"Have you seen the weed?" asks Paul.

"I saw it a few hours ago," I say, but can't seem to locate it now. Never mind that, in our current state, weed is kind of irrelevant.

Rifling through the items on the window shelf on the third floor of Paul's house for the umpteenth time now, we stop to take in the view of the trees that stand tall and proud just outside.

Paul's parents, born-again Christians, have laid a lot of trips on Paul. That he would be a minister, saving people with his missionary work. Though Paul is a great guy, I've never seen him as *that* guy. He likes to get high, listen to rock music, hang out with friends, drink beer, and meet girls.

Our eyes still on the trees, Paul talks about God. I have no idea what he's saying. But I know it's deep.

As he speaks, I notice that the tree branches are geometrically multiplying. I tell Paul that the trees are growing, each branch creating a series of other branches in a frenzy. He sees it too. And is providing commentary, mostly about God, on the nature of the trees.

The proliferation of branches slows down. I feel the inner

world of the tree—its sadness and joys. I live through its ages, from seedling to strapping fifty-foot oak. I'm in the tree's dreams. Its unconscious mind. Or is it in my unconscious mind? Have I crossed a boundary? Did I dip my toe into death? Close to the edge.

When I've been transfixed for, *I don't know how long*, I'm sucked out of that world and back into this one. As if I've been picked up by a giant and thrown across the threshold of another realm. As if the rollercoaster I'm on has just come to an abrupt and powerful stop. When I pull my head back from looking outside the window, Paul does too. Exactly at the same time. We are both absolutely amazed by what has just happened.

"Did you see the tree multiplying and then slowing down?" I ask, panting.

"You mean, did I see the tree moving wildly, its branches flailing and then hypnotically slow down until it became still," he says instantly.

"Yes, exactly."

"What else did you see?"

"I saw the life of the tree. I saw its heart and soul. It spoke to me."

"Do you remember what it said?"

"It spoke to me in feeling. If I could put words into its mouth, it might have said something like HAVE JOY."

Neither of us can believe what we've seen and felt. It's like nothing I've ever experienced. It's like nothing I will ever experience again. I've peered out over the edge of the known world and poked my head into a new and inexplicable one.

After the tree vision, Paul and I become a little hysterical. At one point, when I walk over to the window, almost by accident, he accuses me of going back to see the trees. Memories of the trees' visitation linger. He looks upset, while I laugh at his silly assertion. He wanders over to the window and I accuse him of the same. This time he laughs, and I feel wounded.

We go down to the kitchen to get some Kool-Aid from the fridge. The floor and wall tiles are spotted with green flowers and frogs.

"I've never seen these flowers or frogs in my house," says Paul.

"Maybe the tree and its minions are following us," I say.

We both laugh, uncomfortably.

Paul and I spend many years reflecting on the tree vision. He draws an image of a tree atop a chunk of floating rock. I too draw warped trees with undulating branches and other abstract images. We both draw in tiny strokes, using fine point pencils. We refer to the visions we saw on LSD as the *ancient curves*.

Alchemical Studies

Although I read constantly, I have more books than I can read.

Since I live at home, I'm not eager to leave Greenwich Village after class, unless I must run to my part-time job in Chelsea. I roam the streets, exploring the bookstores, record stores and occult shops.

One day in the East Village I stumble on The Wiccan, one of the oldest occult shops in New York City. I'm intrigued by their extensive collection of tarot cards, occult reliquaries, and books. Their titles include introductions to pagan practices, encyclopedias of the ancient mysteries, guides on crystals, herbs, incense, and of course, books on ufology.

At The Wiccan, I feel a hint of deviance, even though I've been exploring similar ideas since I can remember. At NYU, I'm told by other students that Catholicism is a barbaric occult religion. This is new to me. While I've always been critical of Catholicism, I've never had to defend it to anyone. Having never connected with the ideology of Catholicism, I have, however, been mesmerized by its imagery and sacred relics. Even the far-out ideas of the trinity make sense to me, that father, son and holy ghost are the same being. I like the science-fiction aspects of Catholicism.

As I walk through the store, I pick up a catalog of classes they offer. I love the class names: *The History of Hermes Trismegistus*, *The Esoteric Quest*, *The Art of Dying*, and *UFO Abductions*. I fold the catalog and place it in my bag.

"Are you looking for something?" asks a bearded young man

behind the counter. He's wearing black eyeliner and lipstick. He's dressed in leather and chains, reminiscent of the zombies from the King Diamond concert a few years back.

"Any questions about the classes?"

I don't respond right away. It's an old habit. Growing up in a tough neighborhood, you learn to watch and listen before you talk. Especially when you're in unknown territory.

"We also offer private lessons, if you're interested," he says. "Our resident alchemist, Pedro Millanova, offers a five-session course on esoteric studies."

He pauses, batting his eyes, waiting to get a response from me. I can tell he's gauging me.

"He's in the back room if you'd like to meet him."

I'm a little intimidated by the offer, but I'm also interested.

"Is he often here?" I finally ask.

"He's at our upstate store usually. You got lucky today."

I realize this might be a con. Like drug dealers I knew as a kid: *I got a bag of Thai weed but you gotta buy it now; I'll give you a deal.* I look behind the store clerk to a wall where there are exotic posters of occult imagery: A portrait of The Hanged Man, images of alien beings masquerading as regular citizens in long coats, and Buddhist mandalas.

"I'll come back another time," I say. Old habits die hard. I browse the store a bit more and exit.

A few days later, after class, I walk over to The Wiccan again. The store clerk recognizes me and smiles. I smile back. After browsing the books, I walk up to the counter.

"Hi, I was wondering if Pedro Millanova is in the store today."

"I believe he is," says the clerk. "Let me go check." Now, of course, my radar is up. *Is he really here every day?*

"By the way, my name is Victor," he says when he comes back. I introduce myself and we shake hands. "Pedro is in the back area, where that red curtain is. He says he can see you now if you'd like." He nods his head toward the back of the store. I say thank you and proceed to the back area.

Behind the red curtain Pedro Millanova sits at a table adorned with tarot cards, a large crystal ball and lighted candles. At first, he ignores me. He's gazing into the crystal ball. After thirty seconds or so, he looks up, seeming surprised to see me.

"Please sit down," he says, gesturing at the chair across from him.

"Very nice to meet you," he continues. "I'm Pedro Millanova. I understand you're interested in private classes."

I tell him that Victor described an occult survey class but emphasize that I'm also specifically interested in ufology.

"Yes, of course," says Pedro, twirling his long black mustache. "I have taught many students. In fact, some of them have gone on to be erudite teachers themselves. Some are even famous," he adds. I can detect an accent. Maybe he is Mexican. I am not certain. "But I cannot mention their names; it would be, how shall we say, indelicate."

I don't bite on his last statement. Sounds like the tricksters I knew from the neighborhood.

"Tell me about your background," he continues.

I give him a brief overview of my history and my interests, particularly in ufology.

"Have you ever had a UFO encounter?" he asks, his eyes widening as he speaks. A slight smile creeps across his face but is then replaced by his serious stare. I tell him the truth, that I have seen a UFO.

"I've also been reading Carl Jung at school. I'm very interested in his work," I add.

"Jung, of course. What is it that you like about Jung?" he asks.

"I'm interested in Jung's notion of the collective unconscious. That the collective unconscious is bigger than our rational mind and knows more about us—about the world— than our ego knows."

"Very good, very good."

"I've also read his *Flying Saucers* book, which I find fascinating."

"I see. This is an excellent place to start." He pulls a new copy of Jung's *Alchemical Studies* from a shelf behind him.

"You must make this a part of your reading." Taking the book from him, I notice the blue sapphire ring on his bony finger.

Alchemical Studies is one of the books in my class bibliography. I open it and turn the pages. I'm immediately captivated by the illustrations. Some are reprinted from ancient European and Eastern Philosophy texts. I've always been drawn to pictures with intricate details like this. Some of the illustrations are done by Jung in his attempts to explore his own unconscious. I've drawn images like this as well.

"Very well," says Pedro. "Please take this up front. You can pay for this and our five-session pre-package class. Two hundred and twenty-five dollars. No refunds." He picks up the deck of tarot cards and looks away from me. "I'll see you next week at the same time."

I'm a little stunned by the abrupt ending.

"Any questions?"

"No," I say, though I have a lot of questions. I walk to the counter and pay for the book and the classes.

I read *Alchemical Studies* on the train back to Queens. I'm completely fascinated. Jung thinks that to understand the collective unconscious we must read the works of European occultists like John Dee and Fiddle. Their ideas provide a history, a roadmap to the present state of the collective mind as the archetypes they are concerned with reappear in our time, though perhaps in a different context. Jung says that when alchemy became virtually shunned out of existence, the investigation of the human psyche went undiscovered for several hundred years. It's like we've lost contact with a significant aspect of the mind. Of human experience.

My first session with Pedro begins with meditation. We've moved to a room in a gigantic apartment adjacent to the store. The ceilings are at least twelve feet high. The room is furnished with meditation pillows and couches.

Pedro hands me a book. "You need to read this." The book is *No Boundaries* by Ken Wilbur. "But for now, we will start with breathing. Breathe into your stomach and slowly let your breath out of your mouth." He shows me how he pumps his stomach to direct breath to it. After meditation we again discuss Jung.

"Jung was like a shaman, you see. Other cultures have a lineage of shamans. Their father or mother was a shaman, as was their grandmother and so on. But Jung comes from a family of Swiss ministers. Jung turns modern metaphysics on its head even as he denies that he's a metaphysician. He's a scientist, he claims. According to Jung, life's biggest problems 'can never be solved, but only outgrown.'"

We discuss what I am learning about Jung in school. But Pedro takes me beyond what I'm learning in class.

"Do you think Jung believed in UFOs?" he asks.

"From what I've read it seems like he believed that UFOs are a phenomenon conjured by the collective unconscious."

"Perhaps that is so."

I am impressed by Pedro's knowledge. There is something of the charlatan about him, but he is also very learned.

For my third session, now that I know my way, I go right to the apartment through a series of curtains and closed doors. One passage doesn't have a door or a curtain; it's draped with ruby beads.

When I arrive, Pedro is seated in meditation.

"How free are you?" he asks upon seeing me.

"What do you mean, free?"

"Free in your thinking. Free from the constraints of convention.

"I think I'm pretty free."

"Feel free to take off your clothes. Let go of your boundaries. Then we can meditate."

I'm not sure what this is about.

"Don't worry. It's safe. We're meditating. This is part of the training."

Pedro gets up, takes off his clothes and sits back down.

"See, that was easy. Now you."

I hesitate. *This guy seems mostly real. We're just meditating, right?*

"We're just meditating," he says, like he's read my mind. *What the fuck!*

I stand up, strip my clothes off and sit cross-legged on a pillow. After thirty minutes of meditation, I have a raging hard-on. When we get up to bow to each other, Pedro sees that I have a hard-on. He smiles.

At our final session, Pedro has tarot cards laid out in front of him before I arrive.

"Let us meditate," says Pedro. He takes off his clothes. I do the same.

After meditation, Pedro directs my attention to the tarot cards. We're both still naked. He picks cards up and places them down again. "Do you know what Jung thought of the tarot?" he asks. Since I don't reply, he continues. "Jung saw the tarot as a divine journey of the soul. The tarot charts the process of individuation. How we become our most fully realized selves," says Pedro. "We use tools like the tarot to explore our unconscious. He felt the same about the *I Ching*. Now that our sessions are ending, I'd like to make a few suggestions." He pauses, fingering a beaded necklace which is wrapped around his hand. Now he's whispering a prayer to himself. "I'd like you to challenge yourself. Challenge your prejudices and expectations. I want you to read difficult books. Read things you don't understand." This sounds like good advice. "Before we end. Please come over here. Sit on my lap."

Is he just gay and this is a hook up?

"Look, I'm not gay," says Pedro. "This is part of the training. Going beyond your boundaries." I am doubtful. But I also don't want to be a coward. I walk over to him and stop in front of him.

"Sit down, facing me, in my lap."

He's sitting cross-legged. I sit on top of him facing him.

"Let's breathe together." His breath blows across to me. It is warm.

I'm nervous but close my eyes and breathe to his count. Crossing this boundary has pushed me into a higher state of consciousness, opened a door in my mind. When we come down from the meditation, he says, "OK, open your eyes now." I open my eyes and we stare intently at each other.

"That wasn't so bad, right?"

"No, it wasn't," I say.

As I stand up, Pedro notices that I have a hard-on. I'm a little embarrassed by this. He giggles, then his face is serious. I thank him as I leave. He shakes my hand. We embrace.

I leave The Wiccan that day feeling perhaps Pedro is a phony, but he is serious, too. Maybe he enjoys seeing if he can give younger men a hard-on just to prove it can be done. But I've also read some great books and had some insightful discussions and learned something.

Living for Free

After college, I escape the little fishbowl of my world. I move out to the Bay Area and stay with an old friend, Felicia, for a few weeks in the Oakland hills, until I find a place downtown.

I find a job working at a computer retail store near the University of California, Berkeley, pack all my things and leave the girlfriend I have been living with. She is supposed to join me but decides not to in the end. It's heartbreaking but I must go.

This is the first time I've lived alone. Being on my own in a different state, I worry I'll go crazy, feel too lonely. But I don't. I find myself. I go to meditation centers around the Bay Area. There are Buddhas holding me up the whole time.

Since I work in Berkeley, I walk to the Empty Gate Zen Center atop a small hill near the Berkeley campus. To my Catholic eyes, the prayers and sacred objects of Buddhism seem familiar. Meditating in the Empty Gate Zen Center, for the first time I embrace a spiritual practice. I feel noble sitting on my mat. I am good at it. I can meditate for forty-five minutes, reaching states of emptiness.

I also go to the San Francisco Zen Center in the Haight-Ashbury district. I often drink coffee at one of my favorite cafés before going to the center. Smelling the beautiful fragrances of jasmine and eucalyptus while sipping my coffee, I behold a beautiful vision of the city. Atop the rolling hills on the Haight, with the bay in view, San Francisco looks like a sparkling jewel. The San Francisco Zen Center is gigantic. The old wood floors creak when you walk on them. I feel at home at the Zen Center. I can meditate there for long stretches. But what does it mean to be a good meditator?

At one point, nearly out of money, I talk to Steve, the director of Empty Gate. I have been practicing meditation and attending services, but now I'm entertaining the idea of moving into the center.

"You could live at the center for free," says Steve. Of course, I am interested. "Free room and board," he continues. "But" he adds, the smile fading off his face, "you'll have to work at the center's hospice to take care of people who are basically coming here to die."

"To die?"

"They come here when the hospitals and doctors have given up. You care for them and feed them. You hold their hands."

I nod.

"Do you think you can do this?" he asks.

"Let me mull it over."

After a few weeks of considering my decision, I decide not to move in. I'm not strong enough to be that close to death. I haven't yet achieved those levels of compassion or enough of an understanding of emptiness. My meditation skills mean only so much, it seems.

My brother calls me. "Are you moving back to New York City?"

"I'm planning to," I say.

"If you're planning to, you should move back now," he says.

"What's going on?"

"Dad is dying. He has pancreatic cancer. The doctor says he has three months to live." I hear the words, but I don't hear the words. "You should come back now. You might never see him again," he adds.

I'm broke, but now I have a reason to move back to New York City. I want to see my father. When I get back to New York City, Dad's hair is almost completely white. His mobility shrinks day by day. He spends most of his time in the little bedroom where he used to watch the New York Giants football games. Whereas he would smoke cigarettes watching the games when he was healthy, he now lies down in the bed, connected to an oxygen tank.

Almost to the day, in three months my father is rushed to the hospital when he declines into a coma. My brother and I are tossed about in the ambulance, speeding through the city streets, blue and red lights blinking, its siren screaming for everyone to get out of the way.

On the third day, my father wakes up in the early morning and asks the nurses to call his family. When we arrive, his eyes are watery, his pupils dilated, his face shining and bright. He has something he wants to tell us.

"I was in a deep sleep, unconscious. Then I saw an illuminated portrait of all of you. This portrait pulled me out of the well of darkness I was in. I followed the light until I woke up." Dad is speaking like a prophet, or a poet. His eyes are on fire; there is a little bit of madness in them.

He talks to each of us, one at a time. He is saying goodbye. When he gets to me, he says "I can go from here to Mars, I'll never find anyone like you." I chuckle. It's funny. It's like he says it because I want to hear that. Because that is our connection. Space, space-travel. Time machines.

Tears running down my cheeks, I let go of his hand. When it's my mother's turn, my father asks us all to leave.

Later that night, as the wind gently blows in from the hospital window, having said his goodbyes and salutations, my father's soul departs the earth.

Time Slip

While thumbing through the pages of Philip K. Dick's "Martian Time Slip" at a bookstand on the Upper East Side, I meet a guy who launches into a discourse on Dick's writing and legacy. Kevin has not yet introduced himself. He knows a lot about Dick; I have only read *Man in the High Castle*. I'm curious.

"In the Bay Area, where I'm from, where Dick's from, all of my friends have read Dick," says Kevin, his teeth slightly bucked, his tongue darting out of his mouth in a nervous tick. He speaks like a know-it-all. His right eye socket looks reddened a bit; both eye sockets are cavernous, like he could place a golf ball in each. Kevin has a full head of straight brown hair, he is slightly taller and maybe thirty-five, ten years older than I am.

During this time, Dick's books aren't so well known. Despite the popularity of the movie *Blade Runner*, based on one of his short stories, his cult following is still relatively small and tribal.

"Dick refers to the Bay Area in his stories; he lived in Berkeley," brags Kevin.

"I worked in the neighborhood Dick lived in when I was in California," I counter, trying to get a word in.

"Right on, man."

To Kevin, having lived in California gives me some credibility. I might be worth talking to and not just another asshole New Yorker. After standing at the bookstand for more than an hour, we decide to go to a nearby café. We speak for hours, discover we live a few blocks apart, and start meeting often.

Kevin's from Marin County, so we've both moved to New

York from California. It's like we've crisscrossed some invisible intergalactic highway, missing each other only to find each other at a bookstand on the Upper East Side. The roads that have brought us together started in very different places.

My life is different now that I live in Manhattan. There could be no going back to the insular neighborhood of my youth. The Queens I left is still a working-class borough neighborhood. While there is a huge immigrant population, they mostly stay to themselves.

In many ways, Kevin is everything I want to be: a hippie from California studying for a PhD in philosophy. Kevin and I have a lot in common, despite our vastly different origins and experiences. Aside from our shared interests in philosophy and science fiction, we are both into psychedelia, music, literature, and art, and we both live on the Upper East Side. And we are both single.

Kevin is incredibly well read, knows a lot about film and has a massive music collection. I mean a wall-to-wall music collection, including boxes of unopened CDs and piles of books everywhere. He knows the names of vintage record labels, like Decca, Gennett, Vocalion, and Okeh, and he schools me in them. Kevin buys CDs he already owns when they are newly issued by a record label he loves. He's obsessive. I love his obsessiveness.

"Unlike schools in New York City, Fairfax High School had classes in jazz" crows Kevin. It's hard to disagree with Kevin's comparison of our high schools, though I must therefore admit I had a poorer education than he did. While he was watching foreign films and reading philosophy at Fairfax, I was having a mediocre time at my high school in Queens. We didn't study high level philosophy, jazz, or foreign film. We studied English and math.

"When I was younger, my teachers said that I was the best math student in Fairfax High School," he says one time. Kevin often reminds you of how smart he is.

"But I didn't go to a fancy east coast college like New York University," teases Kevin, "I dropped out of high school because I was too busy following the Dead and taking acid." He watches my reaction. I hardly blink. Old habits.

"I worked while I was in college to pay for it," I say, defensively.

"You Reagan era kids were trained to work hard."

"It's not like I wanted to."

"Sometimes I wish I'd spent my younger years learning a professional trade, like computer programming," he says, as if to give me a backhanded compliment. "I was too busy learning, reading and traveling."

Kevin lived in Jakarta for a few years, then went back to undergraduate to finish his philosophy degree.

I concede the ground to Kevin. The truth is, I wish I had grown up like him. It's not like I wanted to work. I wanted to hang out, read great books and listen to great music too. More than that, I am embarrassed at my lack of education. I meandered my way through voracious reading, my college experience, and emulating the people I respect. When I hear someone or something that I consider worthy, I listen. Kevin is certainly worth listening to.

Sometimes we stay at his place to listen to music from his vast collection. Sometimes we go hear live music. The conversation never stops, though admittedly, it's mostly Kevin talking.

On the walls of his apartment, Kevin posts calendars for the Film Forum, the Village Vanguard, and other music and film venues. He says the real reason he came to study in New

York City is so he could see his jazz heroes perform live. He also records many of the performances. The labeled cassette tapes are stacked on his books, which are placed on boxes that contain more books. Kevin's diligence, taste and knowledge are an education for me.

One night we head out to hear Ron Carter's jazz quartet in downtown Manhattan. Kevin covertly wears a microphone attached to a tape recorder. I have never listened like I do at concerts with Kevin. We don't talk. We sit quietly, our ears wide open. The night we see Ron Carter's band play, I am convinced we are witnesses to another form of intelligence. As if select humans and other intelligences are privy to the highly complex communication Ron Carter offers to the cosmos. As if the venue that night is at the center of the universe, if even for a brief while. There is a quiet during the musical performance, like space-time has folded in on itself. My breath slows as I listen to the music, the slow drip of time rising to my brain. I am not smoking weed at this time in my life.

I buy more drinks than Kevin does. I get the feeling this happens frequently. I'm not sure if Kevin is trying to get over on me. Or is Kevin trying to avoid me getting over on him? This is how a kid from Queens thinks sometimes.

We are both drunk when we get back to his place. We've been discussing John Locke, the English philosopher, and his idea of personal identity, of consciousness. Kevin knows way more than I do and is fresh on the topics. But being a smartass, I challenge him. I rely on common sense. I pose questions and don't offer much in the way of knowledge or answers. Kevin grows hip to my strategy. Not that I've planned a strategy; it's an approach I've learned growing up in the streets. If you say less, the other guy is more likely to trip himself up.

"Well, tell me what you know about Locke," he asks me in a drunken stutter. My answer is short and mostly correct.

Kevin twists his face, like he's disappointed I gave him the right answer. But he wants to challenge me more.

"Tell me how Locke's notion of personal identity is argued in Derek Parfit's *Persons and Reasons*," slurs Kevin, now tipping up on his toes, pointing down at me with his index finger.

"What is this, a test?" I ask, increasingly pissed off.

Kevin leans in, nearly rubbing his big pointy Irish nose on my face. I push him back a little.

"You want to hit me, right?" he asks.

"You're a fucking jerk, man. I don't want to hit you."

"I can tell by the way you're looking at me that you want to punch me in the face."

"No man, you're fucking crazy," I say.

We stare at each other for a bit, then I turn around, open the door and walk away. For a few seconds, it reminds me of the street fight encounters I had growing up in the projects.

Months later we run into each at the Connecticut Muffin on Second Avenue.

"Hey man, I'm sorry if I pissed you off," I say in a gesture of conciliation.

"Yeah, egging you on to punch me was maybe too much," says Kevin.

We shake hands.

"I was never going to hit you," I add.

Kevin points to his eye socket. The socket is bruised and moist, as if continually watered with tears.

"See here, I was having an exuberant disagreement with some New York guy I worked with. After we got heated up, he turned, as if to walk away. Then when I looked away, he turned back and popped me right in the eye. It felt like he knocked my eye out. That would never have happened in California."

That might not happen in California, but in the Queens I grew up in, you would get punched in the face if you pushed someone too far. I could easily see Kevin working someone up, nudging and nudging, refusing to ease up, until some angry guy exploded on him. He blamed this kind of thing on the New York City versus Bay Area dichotomy, but the fact is, he didn't know when to shut up. I liked listening to Kevin; he had a lot to say. But in New York City, in general, people don't often give you the time of day. You have people's attention for a bit and then they're off. And what's worse, Kevin has a thing about being right all the time. No one likes a snot nose who points out when they're wrong. Kevin never figured that out.

"I have only four papers to write," says Kevin, referring to four papers he must submit to achieve all but dissertation (ABD) status in his PhD program.

"Why don't you just get them done?" I say. In a few years, I'll start my MA in English. Kevin's discussions of philosophy help me. I read every book we talk about, adding each one to the stacks on racked shelves and bookcases in my apartment. There are books everywhere.

"Philosophy papers can take years to write," he replies. "They have to be perfect."

"Why don't you write an imperfect paper and hand it in?"

A smile breaks across his face.

"I don't do that, man," he says.

"But you could get it done."

Eventually Kevin drops out of the PhD program.

One evening, listening to Jimi Hendrix's *Axis Bold As Love* in Kevin's apartment, we hear Mitch Mitchell waft over the speakers.

Good evening, ladies and gentlemen. Welcome to radio station EXP. Tonight we are featuring an interview with a very peculiar looking gentleman who goes by the name Mr. Paul Caruso, on the dodgy subject of, Are there or are there not flying saucers or UFOs? Um, please Mr. Caruso, could you give us your considered opinion on this nonsense about spaceships and even space people?

To which Hendrix replies, in a voice modified by special effects.

Thank you, as you all know, you just can't believe everything you see and hear, can you? Now, if you'll excuse me, I must be on my way.

"Thanks for putting this on for me," I say.

"Now I'm going to put on something different," says Kevin, pulling out a collection of music CDs from the library that lines the walls of his apartment.

"I collect old jazz CDs. Anything on the Decca, Okeh, Gennett labels."

Kevin slides a CD out of a jewel case and hands me Red Nichols and His Five Pennies.

The music is sparkling and fine.Quite similar to the early Benny Goodman my father played for me in his car when we listened to the *The Make Believe Ballroom Time* radio program.

I pick up the jewel case and pull out the liner notes. I'm fascinated by the sound of this music. Years later I read about the constellation of musicians who played on each other's albums. Players like Jimmy Dorsey, Bix Beiderbecke, Joe Venuti, Eddie Lang & Benny Goodman. The list goes on.

"I want to hear more. Maybe a different genre."

"What kind of stuff do you like?" asks Kevin.

"String music. Guitar music," I say. "Definitely guitar music."

"I have the perfect thing for you," says Kevin, retrieving a small box of unopened CDs from his bedroom.

"What's this?"

"I bought them from J&R Music. Downtown. They were on sale," says Kevin, pulling out the CDs one by one. "I have them all on vinyl back home in California."

He puts on a CD, then hands me the jewel case with liner notes. The CD is called *Back Home in Sulphur Springs* by Norman Blake.

The guitar plays at lightning speed, but clean and accurately. I would categorize the music as country or bluegrass.

"Why haven't you played this for me before?" I ask. It's kind of a stupid question. How is Kevin supposed to know which CD from his massive collection to play? Like he can read my mind.

I begin to develop my own collection: jazz, bluegrass, Delta Blues, American String Music. My expanding music collection opens my mind and ears. When Kevin and I listen to music, I sink into the music. I close my eyes. I hear more and more all the time. Like my brain is growing. It's as if there are new languages being learned by listening to music. New forms of knowledge and intelligence. It's not just about enjoying the music; it's about hearing the musician's vision, participating in the musician's creation. Like both player and listener are bound together, embracing, whirling around with one another through the music. Music is a form of magic.

A few years later, out of work, out of money, and sick of New York, Kevin moves back to the Bay Area. He leaves me boxes of unopened CDs.

"I might as well leave them with you. I can't ship these back. I'm a completist, but I have these in my mother's garage already." Kevin gives me a highly complex form of technology that I don't yet understand. In that box lies parts of books I'm soon to write.

Books that will fling me across the world and into the future. And further into the world of UFOs.

Tiny Little Truths

It's my first trip to France since I graduated college. I travel from Paris to Bordeaux by train, then by car to Pau and finally, to Lourdes. Ever since St. Bernadette had a vision of Mary in the grotto, tourists have come to Lourdes, some to be healed by its miracle.

I walk on streets crowded with seekers from across the globe, some on crutches, some in wheelchairs, some even on flat beds. They all come in quest of a miracle.

"You see this queue," says Genevieve, my French guide, pointing to the long line of people waiting to pass through the grotto. "They've come to touch the stone where Mary is said to have appeared." The line to enter the grotto seems endless. None in the queue of people returning from the grotto seem to be healed, but none of them look disappointed. Some are wheeled back on beds, their eyes looking heavenward. There is ecstasy even in the failure of the enterprise. One elderly man clutches rosary beads close to his chest, his teeth chattering.

"Bernadette's father was put in prison after she told the local church about her visions," continues Genevieve, as men holding full-sized crosses like a fleet of crusaders walk by.

"She had over thirty visions," she adds, hunching her shoulders and running her fingers through her straight, greasy hair. She sweats heavily in the August heat, her glasses misted from the humidity.

Nestled at the foothills of the Pyrenees, the sun mercilessly rains down in flames on Lourdes, stinging my cheeks.

"Why did they imprison her father?" a German on the tour meekly asks.

"She threatened the authority of the church," Genevieve quickly replies. As she speaks, wayfarers rush by holding banners proclaiming their church affiliations, as if sprung from the Middle Ages.

"Isn't it ironic that mystics and visionaries became the thorn in the side of the church?" she asks. No one ventures a reply.

Many of the visitors elect to not go inside the grotto and instead wait their turn at the fountain outside to bottle the holy water that comes from the spring. I bottle some water to distribute to my family as souvenirs. They accept the ideas of the church without struggle. They are believers, unlike me.

Genevieve continues her lecture on the Catholic leaders who assumed control of Lourdes, expanding it over the years and finally building the cathedral, the various sanctuaries, statues and fountains on the grounds.

"Do you believe that the grotto has miraculous powers?" I say, the question escaping from my lips.

"Of course, I believe. That goes without saying," she says. "You're telling me that you don't feel anything sacred here?"

I bow my head in embarrassment.

"You must have come for some reason," she says. "Or is it just intellectual curiosity?"

She pauses, then says, raising her voice, "Some people come to Lourdes merely to ridicule it. As if this is all a pathetic circus."

An English couple gives me a look of disgust. I sink back into the group, take out a sandwich and quietly eat it as I look on and listen.

The tour ends on a street next to the gift stores. I wander into a shop named "Sacred Gifts." The Mother Marys have their own section. There is a separate Jesus section and an area for prominent saints. As I pick up pendants and effigies, old men and women, some priests and nuns, rifle through the piles. Although the objects are cheaply made, they sparkle. A nun who looks vaguely familiar turns over the trinkets rapidly, emphatically whispering "no" each time, but determined, it seems, to find the one precious pendant among the heap of fakes.

I mimic the nun, rummaging through the bins. She smiles at me, shaking her head. Finally, she picks up an oval locket adorned with an image of Mary clasping her hands in prayer. She holds this one to her face and kisses it. She begins reciting the Hail Mary in Italian, tears coming to her eyes. I go to her. She reaches to take my hands.

"It's okay," she says in broken English with an Italian accent.

"Did something happen?" I ask. "Can I help?"

"I'm fine, little Matteo," she said. "It's just that you don't remember me."

I am hit like a thunderbolt with the realization that this is Sister Alberti from St. Patrick's, where I went to school.

As my face turns red, I hold her hands tighter. I am flooded with fond memories of Sister Alberti. The classroom with the little desks bolted to small wooden chairs. The green, white, and yellow uniforms like Scotch tape packaging. The twisted black face of the Jesus on the crucifix that hung in the center of the classroom. Sister Alberti's pink cheeks and bright, blue eyes. She's aged so much in the past forty years. In science class I asked her about the universe, about creation, about God. She was so patient.

"Yes, of course I remember you, Sister Alberti." We embrace.

"Did you find what you were looking for in Lourdes?" she asks, her eyes wide and moist.

"I'm not sure what you mean, Sister," I say.

"What I mean to say is that now you must believe in miracles," she says.

"Meeting you is a miracle," I say.

"You still can't see what's right in front of you, little Matteo," she says. She hands me the oval locket adorned with an image of the Holy Mary, a perfect replica of the statue that greeted me every morning in front of the entrance to St. Patrick's School so many years ago.

Sapphire Wind

I'm fifty. It's 2016.

"You dream of me less these days," my father says. Even in my dream, I feel guilty, like I did when he was alive. He's been dead twenty-five years.

"You don't call me anymore?" he says, even though we talked earlier in the week. I try to hide my shame, but he can see through it. I am dreaming. My mind is wide open.

"I often think of you."

"I know you do," he says. His cobalt eyes are miniature Earths with blue oceans and white clouds shifting across them. He is more like Neptune than the proud Neapolitan from Little Italy. And he doesn't smoke anymore.

I look around at the world of this dream. We're floating in space. Heavy dark smoke passes us by. It is freezing cold.

"We're at the tilted edge of the solar system," my father says, pointing to a small shadowy object. "That's Pluto."

Pluto hangs like a nebulous smudge in space. I remember that the Voyager mission just recently passed Pluto and is now sailing out into space beyond the solar system.

"But why are we meeting here?"

"I should be asking you that," he says.

We're asking each other questions out of courtesy. Reading each other's minds would feel like our souls colliding. I am obsessively thinking about Voyager missions that we watched together when I was twelve. And now, knowing that the Voyager has left the solar system, my dreams keep returning to the world we once shared. I am saddened that my father and I move further apart as Voyager moves further away.

"I'm so glad I still have these dreams," I tell him.

I know he needs these dreams, too. I see the longing in his eyes. He keeps talking when I see him. He never wants me to leave. I don't leave by choice. The dreams just end.

"What year is it?" he asks.

"It's 2016, November. A week before your birthday."

"I would be eighty-five. A presidential election year."

"You wouldn't believe who won the election."

"Clint Eastwood," he guesses.

"No."

"Don't tell me there's an Italian in the White House."

"There has been a black president. And we did come close to electing Hillary Clinton."

"I can't believe a Clinton lost."

"She lost to Donald Trump," I say, laughing. He knew all along, yet we both laugh hysterically.

"He's a mobster and a fraud."

"You have no idea how insane this has all been."

"I have been seeing a big influx of souls coming to this side."

"2016 has been a tough year on Earth."

"I know," he says. "So many of your heroes are with me now. Musicians."

"Do you still hate their music?"

"They are my link to you. The music you used to drive me crazy with, blasting it from your room."

"And I listen to your music nowadays, too. Sinatra, Benny Goodman."

"Every night I hear Bowie and Cohen. Performing live, mind you."

"Do you talk to them?"

"Of course. They all say that something's gone from your world. There's a terrible darkness, despite the incredible technology and innovation. Bowie told me your music doesn't have the same poetry it once did."

It feels nice to hear him say Bowie.

"You were never into poetry, Dad."

"I am now. This is all poetry," he says, waving his arm to offer the dizzying expanse around us. I'm struck by the truth of this.

"Many left because of Trump's coming," he continues.

"What do you mean?"

"Their life force ebbed away with the surge of Trump."

"I feel it too. Like something awful is going to happen."

"There's something coming soon," he says, with a serious stare. "Before the end of the year."

"Who's next?"

"I can't say," he says. "But it's big. Very big."

"Please, I need to know. Does this have something to do with alien intelligence? Or is there something terrible about to happen?"

"You always were obsessed with the apocalypse," he says, smiling now.

"Will we destroy each other?" I ask. "Nuclear war?"

He looks at me the way he used to. His eyes reflect the worry I feel. This is the father that looked after me. This is the father I miss now. The only person who could read my fears. As a grown-up man, I feel alone in the world without him.

His form begins to turn a crystalline blue, like the surface of Neptune. He dissolves into a thick sapphire wind. The world on the edge of the solar system collapses into a cloud and is sucked up into a hole in the dark.

"Dad!" I call out.

Silence.

I wake up to "Star Man" by Bowie on the radio, my arm stinging from having fallen asleep. A splotch of weakened sun pokes through the curtains in my bedroom. The sky is gray and cold. A drizzle beats against the window. A light wind rattles the half-drawn blinds.

Books as UFOs

I've been collecting books for as long as I can remember. After the library installed sensors and I couldn't steal books anymore, I began buying them. I've refreshed my book collection as my obsessions have evolved from spaceships, mythology, and technology to novels. From outer space to inner space.

I meet Bob while thumbing through Marshall McLuhan's columns in East Village Books.

"Do you like McLuhan?" he asks. I nod.

"I was his archivist." He directs me to a page in the *Gutenberg Galaxy* and quotes an extensive passage.

I have been reading McLuhan's books over the past year. He clearly knows a lot about McLuhan.

Bob looks about fifty-five but says that he is seventy-five and tells me he and his wife have invented an elixir that keeps them young. Bob is an amazing bullshit artist, but he is extremely well read and knowledgeable. I try not to focus on whether he tells the truth. I just listen to his stories.

In graduate school a new deluge begins. English literature books pile to the ceiling. It's dizzying. My then wife, Natalie, like me, is on a reading frenzy, studying for her PhD in Russian literature. We are eventually buried in books, even to the point where we can't find each other. Am I under that heap, or this one? Where am I? For a Milton class, I read every book on Milton I can find, even if I don't like the book. I'm deranged, obsessed. I enter a new phase of Nordic mythology research, picking up used books from stores on the Upper West Side that have a section devoted to it. I sleep at the bottom of an ocean of books.

When Natalie and I split up, my books, along with every-thing else, go into a storage facility. Boxes upon boxes of books. I can't remember which books I have. My sadness is locked away in those books. Like abandoned lonely children, they await their fate in silence. My heart bleeds.

A foggy year or two later, when I empty out the storage room, I sell most of the literary criticism books. I'll never read them again.

At some point, I read books related to psychedel-ics. Psychedelics and philosophy. Psychedelics and cosmos. Psychedelics and meaning. Another pillage accumulates. As does another bookshelf, now in the bedroom. I sit atop the rubble, happy and silly. Laughing. There is insurmountable joy in receiv-ing, reading, and collecting these books. They are like a rainbow bridge to eternity. My own personal connection to the cosmos. I can reach out and grab Saturn. I can caress distant stars. Hold galaxies in the palm of my hand.

The more I read, the less I can retain, the less I seem to know. It's as if I read because my mind is devoid of independent thought. I am like a dragon under the mountain who needs to be fed books just to stay alive. I am pathetic. Ridiculous. But I can't help it. Books are one of the few refuges of my life. I want to die mid-sentence reading a book, so I'll never notice. Perched on my hand, a book is the most beautiful thing I can imagine. Sometimes better than sex. And longer lasting.

Casino UFO

A few weeks ago, my eighty-two-year-old mother, Cookie, fell face first into the wall at home, seriously wounding her collarbone. She didn't tell anyone. Days later my sister, Patty, saw the purpled bruise streaking down from her shoulder and across her chest.

"What's this?" Patty said, lifting the part of Cookie's shirt that covered the bruise.

"It's nothing."

"Nothing? Mom, please, tell me what happened," pleaded Patty. Cornered, Cookie confessed.

At this point, we're not sure whether Cookie wants to live. Patty and Paolo and I take turns calling her, visiting her, taking her out, taking her away. Anytime we see her could be the last time.

I call to ask if she wants to go away for Labor Day. "Do you want to go the beach at Montauk?" I ask. "They still have available rooms," I add, knowing she probably doesn't want to go. She's silent. "Mom?"

"I don't think so," she says. In Montauk she'd be stuck peering out at the world from the keyhole of a hotel room. As it is, she's home almost every day, though still working one day a week. Work is her last grip on the outside world. She is at war with the seasons. Her unsteady feet can slip on the ice. The summer promises skies of hell flames.

"Do you think we can book something at Atlantic City?"

I'm nauseous just imagining the melody of slot machines,

noise, and smoke. With Labor Day only a few days away, I doubt we'll be able to book a room.

"Let me see if I can get a complimentary room," says my mom, coughing into the phone. She knows all the reps at the Tropicana. They give her free lodging in return for the money she spends at the tables. Before she hangs up, I hear the clinking of ice in her glass.

The next day Cookie calls me. Not only has she received a complimentary two-night stay with two beds, the Tropicana offers her dinner for four at PF Chang's.

On the way to Atlantic City, she is quiet, sitting in the back seat next to my son, Isaac. "Are you okay back there?" I ask, looking at her in the rearview mirror. Her eyes are four times their normal size behind the lenses of her glasses. My wife, Mariella, tries to talk to her, turning around in her seat. Cookie doesn't answer much. This isn't like her.

"Stop for a cigarette?" I ask, after driving about one hour into New Jersey. I know her nerves are rattled from not smoking.

Stepping out of the car, the scorching September sun pours on my face, heavy and thick like lava. I smell the burning tires from the highway.

My mother swings the car door open on her side before I can open it for her. The door smacks back on her. Normally this wouldn't matter. But in her case, her bones weakening, more brittle every day, the door is a weapon. I should have rushed to open it. I can hear my brother's panicked voice in my head, "That's why you need to get the door for her." Paolo follows her around nervously, a madcap butler holding her arm, helping her.

"I'll do it myself," Cookie shouts at him. He ignores her shouts and never lets her go.

Back in the car, Cookie says that the door left a black and

blue mark on her ankle. We must be prepared for anything. Driving down the narrow road to Atlantic City, I see the shiny golden buildings and glittering facades. The skyline looks like a heap of fake gemstones.

Checking in at the Tropicana, I get a first glimpse inside of Atlantic City. There's a husband and wife standing in line, arguing.

"What the hell do you want from me?" the husband shrieks. "I told them I don't got no more money for them to come."

"They're my cousins," his wife says. She has a red beehive hairdo. An oversized gold cross hangs from her neck. "You said you was gonna invite them."

The husband grumbles. The hotel lobby reminds me of the Off-Track Betting places my father took me to as a child. Faces sweat with worry, their worn clothes, two decades out of fashion, saggy and defeated. The old worries about my father's gambling come back to me. My parents' anxiety about not having enough money to pay the rent. Being sent to the auditorium with the other school kids whose parents didn't pay tuition. Knocks on our apartment door from people in long coats, their faces hidden under hats. My mother haranguing my already beaten down father. Night after night.

"Smoking or non-smoking?" the hotel clerk asks.

"Non-smoking, please," I answer. "Sonofabitch," my mother says. "You're such a phony. I can't believe you."

"Please Mom. I can't breathe in a smoking room."

"No one smoked like you."

"That was thirty years ago." She's never forgiven me for quitting. "What about Isaac?" She doesn't respond.

Cookie takes the access card and gives it to me, her hands shaky and tense. I fight my guilt; I'll never get a wink of sleep in a smoking room.

We head to the room to drop off our luggage. I hold my mother's arm and warily guide her through the hotel corridors.

Patty has told me to drop my mother at the casino then head to the beach.

"You can pick her up later," Patty said. "If you left her in the casino for a week straight, she'd be fine. You come back and she'd still be there smoking a cigarette, drinking a scotch." I don't like the idea of dropping her off at the casino. It's like I'm dropping off my child with a psychotic babysitter.

Unlike me, Mariella doesn't nitpick about my mother's edginess, or about mine either. She guides us to the casino, knowing I will only get us lost.

"Take me to the Wheel of Fortune," my mother says. "That's where the action is." We walk deeper into the casino, passing a lady with gold teeth carrying a bag that looks like it contains everything she owns. A man sucks on his cigarette, his eyes rheumy and swollen. He looks like he hasn't slept. Like he drinks until his liver gushes with blood every night.

"Not here," my mother says.

I don't like anything about this place. I can't breathe. My heart feels knotted. There is a constant din of noise. Amid the jingles and rings of the casino machines erupt the screams of winners and losers, outcries of woe, and loud moans. I am trapped inside a deranged arcade, blinded by the flashing multicolored lights and assaulted by the deafening ring of the slot machines. I hope out of nowhere a cliff will appear that I can fall off of, sending me to my death. I'll welcome it with open arms.

We keep walking into rooms nested in still other rooms. When we finally find the Wheel of Fortune, my lungs feel like rusty engine parts.

"This is it," my mother says, pointing to the machine. We walked all this way, and it looks like all the others. I help Cookie sit down next to a woman drinking scotch from a plastic cup. The woman's eyes spin with wheeling flames, reflecting the wheels on the slot machine. One seat over, a man with one eye open pulls the slot handle without looking at the machine. There are cigarettes squashed in ashtrays, rows of bottles, and near empty plastic cups, some filled with cigarette butts.

"Are you sure?" I ask my mother, before leaving her in this miserable ditch of hell. I am dizzy from the lack of oxygen, the blaring sounds and flashing lights.

"This is perfect," she says. "Go to the beach. I'm fine."

I stay, waiting for her to start playing. Mariella doesn't rush, either. She's strong like my mother. She takes all of this in stride, looking at me to see if I'm upset, managing everyone's terrors in her soundless way.

A waitress roughly my mother's age comes to take her drink order. She hobbles away in high-heeled shoes, hardly able to walk.

"Go already," Cookie barks suddenly. Then softly, "It's nice out and you'll enjoy the beach."

Mariella and I linger.

"I said go," she says sternly now.

Mariella nods at me, motioning to leave. Isaac trails behind us. The last thing I see is the back of Cookie's little head.

"I'm shocked," I say to Mariella.

"I can imagine," she says.

"After all we went through with my father's gambling," I say, "and she wants to gamble."

"She likes to gamble. It makes her happy," says Mariella. "This is Cookie's heaven and your hell. The smoking I can do without."

"I hate the smoking."

Later that night, at PF Chang's, we order drinks. My son hides under the table. I can't see him, but it bothers me that he's probably crawling in piles of greasy fried rice and sticky puddles of soda.

Cookie is smiling. The drinks, smoking, and gambling have calmed her. Looking at the menu, she says, "I'll order. I know what to get and I want to have a taste of everything."

It's easier if Mariella and I just agree. Cookie tells Mariella that she started going to casinos in the Bahamas when my grandmother was dying of cancer. They went to an alternative cancer center in Freeport. That's where Cookie started drinking and gambling. Now, holding Mariella's hand, Cookie recalls her own mother.

"She was a special woman. Never one to complain. And good to the core. Right?" she gestures towards me.

"She was like Gandhi," I say, half-jokingly.

"I don't know about that," my mother says. "She was giving and kind. And when she got sick … I'm going to cry now." She pauses, takes a breath. "When she got sick, I couldn't let go," she says, swallowing her words. I reach out and hold Cookie's hand. She doesn't cry easily.

"I couldn't let her die." Her words weigh on us. Isaac climbs into my lap and rocks back and forth, playing with my glasses.

"I couldn't let her die, not so much for her," she repeats, wiping teardrops from her eyes, "but for me." Now we are all crying. The release is like a downpour after a hot day.

After dinner, we walk my mother back to the casino. Mariella takes us back to the Wheel of Fortune where Cookie finds her lucky machine. An overweight woman is sitting next to my mother's machine, enveloped in a cloud of smoke, breathing out of the folds of her neck. She smiles as we approach.

I help Cookie sit down. She immediately lights a cigarette, blowing the smoke in my face. Isaac starts banging on the machine, pressing buttons randomly. Immediately, guards rush over to us.

"Children aren't allowed to play the machines," one of the guards says, talking into his walkie-talkie, rushing at us. Another guard hurries towards us. I don't know what's happening. Knocking the fire from her cigarette, my mother says it's not legal for kids to even touch the machines.

"I hate this place," Isaac whines. "There are no games for kids." He can only look at the blinking lights. It's like an amusement park with rides he can't go on.

"We'll pick you up a little later," I shout to my mother over my shoulder as we're escorted out by the casino police.

Mariella, Isaac, and I escape to the boardwalk. It's a cool night. The air feels fresh, especially after fleeing the haze of the casino. There are electronic billboards displaying ads and music videos. Even the outside rings with its own din.

Mariella and I know we must do something for little Isaac. He's been locked in cars and hotel rooms. We take him to a video arcade. He pounces on a car racing video machine, punching the controls, wildly spinning the wheel. Isaac smashes into other cars, drives off cliffs into bodies of water. He thinks the point of the game is to get into accidents and drive off the road. Mariella and I laugh until tears run down our faces.

A few hours later, Mariella and Isaac head up to the room and I go in search of The Wheel of Fortune to get Cookie. I'm lost walking through a maze, blinded by the alternating lights and smoke. For a moment I feel panic. I'll never find her. Every slot machine looks the same. I see the people gambling with their last dollars, maybe some have sold valuable possessions to keep playing. This looks like the waiting room for the dying.

I finally find Cookie sitting next to a man with a cane. His hair is wispy and gray. His eyes, fierce and strange, are covered with cataracts. He is blind. How is he playing?

My mom doesn't notice me. She is in the innermost core of the casino. In her left hand she holds a scotch in a plastic cup. With her right hand, she pulls the lever on The Wheel of Fortune. The slot machine now shimmers like an altar, its brassy surface glittering and fiery.

Through the dense smoke, I see a squadron of angels girdle her majestic seat. My mother has said that time slips away when she gambles. When she pulls the handle, she is plunged back in time. Cookie is now thirty years old and with my father again. Her face is smooth, her hair is dark black. She and my father are on vacation in Florida. Now she is pregnant with my sister, her lips cherry red, her brown eyes on fire with life. Now Cookie is by my father's side in the hospital. He is dying. The hole that my father burned into my mother's soul with the pain of his gambling has become the vehicle through which she can visit him.

Suddenly, the smoke from the cigarettes balls up in my lungs and explodes. I cough. The scene comes to an abrupt halt. I have disturbed the magical forces at play.

"Hi Mom, having fun?" I say, now standing over her, my hand over my mouth to hide my gagging. She points to the cards on the screen.

"Nothing, see?"

I don't follow the game. I don't know three-card rummy or poker or any card game really besides solitaire. I am drawn to tarot cards. The Fool. The Magician. The Hermit. The Hanged

Man. I prefer magicians, shamans, and gypsies to gamblers. Maybe they're all gamblers anyway.

My mother presses the button to refresh her hand.

"Nothing again."

I can tell she's had too much to drink.

"So, are you ready to come up?"

"In a little while," she says

"Have you won?"

"Not tonight." She resumes pressing the button, dealing her a new hand. She keeps losing. A gigantic chandelier over the casino shimmers, sending a warm light that penetrates the freezing air conditioning.

When she's ready to leave, I lift her. There's no way she can walk on her own back to the room in this condition. This woman is like a mountain—stubborn and powerful, with marshy soft parts and deep dark caverns. Everyone around her has died. She holds onto life with a grip that whitens her knuckles and rattles her knees. She hates winter and summer and in turn they are fearful of her. They lie waiting for her to stumble. Cookie is subsumed by a world that has been left behind. She is a tribe, a history of her family, fiercely clinging to this world. She is heavy in my arms. It feels as if I am lifting a piece of the earth.

Flickering Lights

One morning I wake up to the sound of a loud boom. I run to the window in my bedroom. The sky is bright blue. I can't see a single cloud. My eyes fix on a squadron of gigantic metallic spaceships zigzagging across the sky in formation.

Outside looking up alongside my neighbors I can see that the ships are black triangles enclosed in translucent spheres. The edges of the triangles push up against the spheres. The ships are massive, like mountains or gods. They move effortlessly and without sound.

A woman taps me on the shoulder. "Do you know why they're here?" She has red hair; her blue eyes are wet with excitement. *She might be wild,* I think to myself.

"No, I don't," I reply calmly.

"They've finally come to take over. They've been watching for thousands of years. They know who we are," she says.

"How do you know this?"

"They've always come to me in dreams. We've fucked up on this planet and now they want to remove us and secure Earth before we make it uninhabitable."

The heavens are exploding, clouds billow and enlarge. Bright lights stream down on us. I'm not sure if they are from the spaceships or what.

On the street it's pandemonium. Cars have stopped, people have gotten out of their cars to gaze into the illuminated skies.

"We didn't take care of Mother Earth," the woman says. "We've been too focused on greed and plundering the bounty we were given."

"Is this a punishment?" I ask.

"It is a reclamation," she says.

I look down and notice that I'm in my underwear.

The sky has become pitch black. Lights flicker and blink. Despite what this woman is saying about the end of the world, the whole thing is beautiful. I feel joyous.

At least we'll all die together, I think. *Isn't that the best way for us to go? In one fell swoop.*

The black fold of night is on fire with erupting stars. The light is so great it shines like its day.

I start to run and bump into Mickey Ness and Squid. Wait, how old am I? When is this happening? I have slippers on, too. Underwear and slippers. I must be dreaming. So I launch myself into the sky, grabbing onto one of the spaceships. Inside the sphere, the black triangle is marked with hieroglyphics that resemble transistors. These are poems about the distances between stars, about the formations of life that have occurred throughout the universe. They are very personal. Reading them, I feel the individual lives of unfamiliar beings coursing through my body. My heart beats with many hearts. I hear music like I heard as a kid in church. The light, sound, and frequency sing in unison like a billion angels in a million heavens.

I've been having this dream all my life.

Making Contact

The year is 2020. COVID has us all trapped in quarantine. Being boxed in our little Brooklyn apartment is beginning to wear on me. I get up before everyone and go out for a walk. It's 5 a.m., no one is on the street. Still dark. There is an eerily still, except for the boisterous bird chirping, which ricochets off the sky, as if this piece of Brooklyn is in a bottle. My nose fills with the smell of the ocean only a few miles away at the end of Coney Island Avenue.

Our neighborhood, Midwood, is residential, with tree-lined streets and big-porched houses, some with flowered gardens. Midwood, derived from the Middle Dutch word, Midwout, meaning *middle woods*, was what the settlers of New Netherland called this area of dense woodland midway between the towns of Boswyck (Bushwick) and Breuckelen (Brooklyn).

Even this early, I'm thinking about my workday schedule. Despite the chaos of the pandemic, I'm still busy taking meetings, talking to clients, and writing reports.

An odd mixture of light from the streetlamps and the breaking sunrise casts a yellowed glow. I look up at the sky to see if the blue orbs will make a showing. Nothing.

From a distance, I see something standing in the middle of the street. Whatever it is, it's not on the sidewalk; it's right in the center of the road. Perhaps it's a traffic cone, blocking cars from entering. Maybe there is construction going on. Even as I get closer, I can't make out what it is. Now I see that it's not orange like a traffic cone; it's white and slightly gray. It's moving.

"Is someone out there?" I say, continuing to approach who-ever or whatever it is.

Something whirs above me. Three blue orbs zip across my field of vision, moving too fast for me to focus on them. I rub my eyes and focus again on the thing in the street, moving sideways as if that will help me protect myself should whatever it is rush at me.

Can it be so? What? As my eyes begin to focus, I see a three-and-a-half-foot-tall owl standing sentry smack in the middle of the street. I slow down, approaching him cautiously. He's snow-white and speckled with grayish dots. His eyelids open and close like shutters; he scrapes the ground with his claws, clenching. I should probably be scared but I'm not. This creature can claw my eyes out of their sockets or pull a chunk of flesh from my body. Yet, I'm in awe of his beauty. I continue sideways toward him. We stare at each other. His eyes glow cobalt as if backlit. I chuckle, if a tad nervously. I've entered the owl's domain and he's not going to yield. The owl's sharp eyes suggest a high intelli-gence, certainly higher than mine. A mind as old as the universe. I'm just a silly human, unable to comprehend the wild things of the world.

Bored with me, the owl swivels his head a full three hundred sixty degrees. He shutters his eyelids again, spreads his wings, nearly eight feet from end to end, and flies off. I watch him soar up into the sky. Three cobalt blue orbs trail the owl.

Fungi as UFO

With only a few nights left of our summer vacation in Greenport, I ask Mariella if she wants to take mushrooms. I've been saving them for a special occasion. Surviving several months of lockdown is a special occasion.

"Mushrooms? Now Matteo?" she asks.

"I got them from Alex," I say. "I thought we could take them when the time was right."

Looking down at my hands, I pause for an answer.

"Is the time right?" I ask.

Still no answer. I keep talking.

"I think this is a good time. I feel cleansed, calm. Do you?"

"I've had a good time, but I'm not sure about the mushrooms."

"Maybe we could ask Rachel if we can drop Isaac off at night and return the favor." We debate this for a bit; I begin to think it's hopeless.

"Why don't we take the mushrooms tomorrow night," says Mariella. "Tonight, we'll take Sammy out and maybe have him sleep over, if Rachel's okay with that."

I'm thrilled. I'm still not sure if she'll go through with it, but I'm feeling more hopeful. I nod and don't say anything. I don't want to mess it up.

The next night, we drop Isaac off at Rachel's. We're alone once again. We head back to our rental apartment. "This will take about thirty minutes to an hour to kick in," I say as I hold a mushroom stem and head in my hand, dividing it into two equal portions.

"Maybe I'll do half of what you're doing."

"Sure," I say, thinking this makes sense.

"But before we take it, let's use our time well," says Mariella, pulling off her shirt.

In a matter of seconds, I'm showing my excitement for her in my pants. That's the life of a parent; you learn to use opportunities as they arise.

After we have sex and get dressed, I say, "Let's go for a walk first. It's a beautiful night. We can take the mushrooms when we're out eating and wend our way home. By the time we get back to the apartment, we'll be tripping." As I say it though, I worry that I might not be able to find my way home on mushrooms. Being escorted home by Greenport police while I chant *Hare Krishna Hare Rama* at the top of my lungs would be terribly embarrassing—for Mariella.

After dinner, we stroll around Greenport until the mushrooms kick in. If the town looks garlanded with tinsel on marijuana, it is completely in flames on mushrooms. The neon signs on the restaurants blur and trail as I swivel my head.

"Do you see that?" I ask Mariella.

"See what?"

"The trail of cobalt blue light coming from the neon sign?" I say, laughing.

"I think you took more than I did," she says. "I'm feeling something though. It's light and soft, like a pretty breeze caressing my body."

"I feel that too, a million tiny fish swarming my body, protecting me. There's an energy flowing up and down my spine, exploding sometimes in spurts of pure ecstasy."

The apartment, when we arrive, is decorated in a rainbow glow. There are bands of color on the walls, colors of forever running in redness and blueness. I know this is the mushroom giving me a glimpse into the inner life of the apartment and its cosmic history. How each particle in the wall was formed, its journey since its inception inside of a star billions of years ago.

I start to tell Mariella what I am seeing, but I lose my train of thought. We both laugh at my ridiculous babbling.

Mariella is standing before me. She's so pretty. She has a long thin nose and big bright blue eyes. We hold each other's gaze for a bit, her arms around my shoulders and my arms around her waist. We smile.

"Your eyes are like oceans," I say. This doesn't really come out the way I mean it.

"Oceans?"

"Yes, but you're a ground creature. You're not a fish."

"A fish? What are you talking about?"

"What I'm trying to say is that you're more like a bird than a fish."

"Really?"

"You're not going to believe this," I say.

"I'm afraid to ask."

"You look like an owl."

"An owl? Well, that's actually kind of cool."

"Yeah, a beautiful owl, with terrifically big, perfectly blue eyes. Look, see the way you just blinked?"

She laughs. And I laugh.

"I think I need to look at you more often. I can learn so much from doing just that."

"Listen, don't get too weird on me, ok?"

Now we're doubling over with laughter.

I put on a Grateful Dead mix, knowing she'll like it too.

"Are you feeling it?" I ask.

"Oh yeah."

I lean my head back on the couch. I'm seeing owls everywhere. I even see one pruning its feathers with its beak and clawing its spiked talons, but I'm not afraid.

I'm privy to a gathering of owls; I've been invited. Some are blue, some are snow-white, some are multicolored. Some glow as if illuminated by the bright lights of a spaceship. The owls communicate with each other in music. I can understand what they are saying.

One owl comes forward. It is snowy white, speckled with gray and black spots here and there, about three-and-a-half feet tall. Majestic, kingly. It resembles Mariella, particularly in the eyes, a hybrid of Mariella and the owl I saw on the street months ago.

"I am your guardian angel," the owl says.

"Come on, Mariella," I say to the owl, thinking it is Mariella in disguise.

The owl ignores my comment and, as it flies away, takes me with it in a swirl of wind. Suddenly, I'm flying way above the earth. Like ten thousand feet high. I can see whole towns, treed areas, and rivers. I fly with the owl, the cool air on my face. The owl's feathers ruffle as it moves in the sky.

"You see that below?" says the owl, pointing to a few scattered towns. "This is how we see your cities and towns. While you're concerned with your house, your town, your nation, we see rivers that connect with other bodies of water. We see how the waters flow under the surface of the earth. And look there. See that patch of trees and how it looks exactly like that other patch of trees a few miles away? To us, it's one forest. The forest in the town. The forest in the city. The forest in the parks."

I'm beginning to think that this owl is not Mariella after all.

This is either some fascinating being from another realm, or I'm just tripping. Or both.

"When you all can see that the earth is one connected being, you will be free."

We drop one hundred feet in one swoop.

"When you see each tree individually, each bird and insect, you will finally have arrived as a species."

The rows of shining green trees and sparkling rivers below me breathe and heave like one heart.

"When you can't bear the sight of even one lonely tree hemmed in on all sides by a tiny square concrete prison and demand its release, you will understand that you need us more than we need you."

Alighting on the ground, the owl takes one step.

"When you realize that trees, rivers, and all people require love, you will know your purpose."

As a great wind blows over us, the trees shake and swirl, their leaves flutter and cheer. Opening my eyes, I find myself standing once again in front of Mariella.

As I've been a little crazy all night, I'm hesitant to tell her what I've just seen.

"Are you going to say something?" asks Mariella.

"I can't remember what I was going to say."

"You started talking and then just stood there and stared at me."

"How long was I staring?"

"At least a minute."

"Was it weird?"

"I'm getting used to it being weird with you in this pandemic. It's all been weird."

The next day, we go hiking at Orient Beach State Park in

Greenport. Located on the eastern tip of the North Fork of Long Island, Orient Beach State Park has a waterfront with 45,000 feet of frontage on Gardiner's Bay and a rare maritime forest with red cedar, blackjack oak trees, and prickly pear cacti. On the trail we see great blue herons, egrets, black-crowned night herons, and spot an osprey perch.

"How long are we going to be here?" asks Isaac. He just wants to get this over with.

"Probably about an hour," says Mariella. "Enjoy the fresh air! And stop thinking about getting back online. You have to take a break from the video screens."

Isaac frowns.

We head out. It's good to escape the blistering heat of the sun. The tree breezes feel soothing. I watch the leaves flapping in the wind, as if they are talking to me. Having been inside so often recently, I gaze up at the sky. It's clear and bright. A few clouds hang suspended in the air. Their whiteness glitters with the sun's light.

Up in the trees, we hear a spotted sandpiper. I'm getting good at identifying birds by their calls. I can tell because of the continuous *weet* notes. *Weet, weet, weet, weet, weet, weet, weet, weet, weet, weet.* Sensing that we've invaded its territory, the spotted sandpiper makes a metallic *spink* sound, telling us not to come any closer. I have my field guide out, looking up at the bird and then down at the pages.

As we're picnicking on lettuce and tomato sandwiches, a forest ranger approaches.

"How are y'all doing?" the ranger says.

"Good," I say. "Good."

"Just want to let you know that the park is closing early today. New pandemic hours."

"That's too bad," says Mariella.

"Sorry to have to cut your hike short," the ranger says.

"We know it's your job," says Mariella. I notice them taking each other in.

"What's your name?" Mariella asks, somewhat flirtatiously, I think.

"Nancy. Nice to meet you."

Nancy is about the same height as Mariella. She has dark hair and a curvy body. Very pretty. I suddenly feel jealous and out of place.

"Hey, Isaac," I say, "come over here." Wandering away, I plan to test my newfound knowledge of bird and tree species. "Let's go see if we can identify birds." Isaac drags himself toward me. Hiking is torture, birding is worse.

Don't tell me she's trying to pick up Mariella, I think. And Mariella seems open to it. More than anything, I feel a little annoyed. I take my pouting with me, as Isaac and I crunch the leaves and twigs on the park floor, walking away from the picnic tables into a canopy of trees.

While I'm talking to Isaac, I keep tabs on Mariella and Nancy. They're less than six feet from each other, I think sullenly. At least they're not embracing, I say to myself. Thirty minutes later they're still deep in conversation, discussing fungi and mushrooms.

"You can find mushrooms in this park," says Nancy, throwing her hair back a bit as she speaks.

"Matteo is a big fan of mushrooms," says Mariella, eyeing me.

"That's interesting," says Nancy.

I try not to take the bait. I'm not sure if they're making fun of me or what.

"I love mushrooms, but they get all of the credit," Nancy says. "I like the funky fungi. The kind of stuff that wraps in threads. The loom. We call it mycelium."

"See Matteo," says Mariella. "You guys can talk about fungi; your favorite topic." Mariella's teasing me as I've become more and more interested in nature.

Finally, I speak up.

"I read that the largest living organism on earth today is a fungus in Oregon just beneath the ground, covering about 3.7 square miles and weighs like thirty-five thousand tons."

"I like a man who knows his fungi," says Nancy. "Pardon the pun." We all laugh a little.

"Are you a fungus expert?" I ask.

"I'm studying types of fungi for my PhD."

"That's what we were talking about, Matteo," says Mariella. "Especially the kind of fungi we had the other night."

I can tell that Nancy gets the allusion to our trip the other night. I'm not sure where this is all going. I'm both jealous and excited that Mariella is flirting with her.

"Why fungi?" I ask Nancy.

"Fungi is the coolest stuff on the planet. It quietly runs the show, connecting everything to everything. It breaks down organic matter, transforming it to soil. Before there were any animals, the earth was covered in gigantic fungi.

"And when they're not eating rock, making soil, digesting pollutants, nourishing and killing plants, producing food, making medicines, manipulating animal behavior, and influencing the composition of the earth's atmosphere, they are doing to people what they did to you the other night." I blink, waiting for her to complete her thought. "Inducing visions, I mean."

"We'd love to learn more about fungi," says Mariella. She

looks at me and back at Nancy. "What are you doing later tonight? Maybe we can get together for dinner." After a pause. "We have a patio. We could sit six feet away."

Nancy nods affirmatively, handing Mariella a business card with the green leaf insignia on it.

"I'd love that; text me later. Anyone who wants to talk about fungus is my friend." As Nancy walks away, Mariella looks over at me again. "She's very nice, right?"

"Yes, she's very nice."

"Kind of cute, too. No?"

"Very cute," I say.

"She's working on how fungi are being explored to prevent pandemics."

"Are you sure you're not just into her?"

"I'm not going to lie. She's very attractive. But I'm really interested in learning more about how fungi might prevent a pandemic."

"Is tonight going to get weird?"

"It depends on what you mean by weird. If having two beautiful women take your clothes off and kiss you all over is weird, then maybe you're the weird one."

My face reddens.

"Joking."

"It's not safe to breathe the same air. We don't know where she's been or who she's been with," I say.

"She's coming over to talk about fungi, my love. Fungi."

That night, Nancy arrives in a tight red dress and fancy shoes. If she looked good before, she looks very sexy now. "This is for you," she says, handing me a bottle of white wine.

"This should go great with the fish and salad," says Mariella.

"And what grade are you in?" asks Nancy, turning her

attention to Isaac.

"Nine," says Isaac, not showing much interest in her question.

"Isaac, when someone asks you a question that means they're interested in you. You should be interested back."

"What grade are you in?" asks Isaac. And now the joke's on us.

"I'm in the twentieth grade," says Nancy, smiling. "I've been in school for as long as I can remember."

Isaac sizes her up, trying to determine if she's telling the truth. Nancy picks up on it.

"I'm studying for an advanced degree in science," she says, her eyes bright and shiny.

"My dad likes science."

"Science is a good thing to like," says Nancy, nodding her head over at me. I smile back at her. "Science has taught us how amazing fungi is, for example."

"How are fungi so amazing?" Isaac asks, stretching the "a" in the word amazing, mimicking Nancy.

"Well, where do I begin? Did you know that penicillin comes from fungi? And that penicillin has saved a lot of lives?"

"I didn't know that."

"Did you know that some scientists believe our ancient forests have cultivated fungi to ward off invasive bacteria? Scientists think that fungi might help us prevent more pandemics like the one we're experiencing now."

After a time, Isaac slinks away to play on his smartphone.

"Great kid," she whispers, once he's out of sight. "Smart and handsome, just like his dad," she adds.

I blush. I get up to open the wine bottle in the kitchen, leaving Nancy and Mariella on the patio. When I return, we continue talking, sharing histories, stories. I must admit, Nancy is cool. She's smart and funny.

"So, what got you into all this?" I ask Nancy.

"Well, I grew up in the Bay Area, California. My father was a forest ranger, and my mother was a science teacher. We went camping a lot. My parents taught me to love nature. They taught me how to slow down time and take in the little moments."

"That's interesting," says Mariella. "My parents took us camping, but I can't say they were scientists. My mother belongs to the garden club and knows a lot about botany. My father loves to garden."

They both look at me, waiting for a response. "I grew up in the city. I never noticed trees or birds or anything. Well, once I noticed what the life of a tree was like." I stop and smile. "But I was on mushrooms."

"See," says Nancy. "Fungi. Perhaps the mushroom experience was the future you, reaching out to your younger self. A way of planting a seed for your eventual transformation." For a split second, she resembles an owl.

Waiting to see if she's joking, Mariella and I look at each other with a smile.

"I'm kind of not joking, but I know it sounds weird."

"A little weird," I say, "but interesting."

After dinner, the sun starts to dim, hiding behind the trees. We've had a few drinks.

"These are lovely trees," says Nancy, pointing out to an area beyond the patio. Some of the trees are at least sixty feet tall, some are smaller with knobbed green, brown roots bulging out of the ground.

"When I was a kid, my father used to tell me to talk to the trees."

"Do they talk back?" Mariella asks.

"If you talk to the trees, you have to imagine them talking back. You must think with your heart, not your analytical mind. It's not a science thing; it's a feeling thing."

"Are you making up what they say back?" I ask.

"No, I wouldn't say that. You look at the leaves, the way they flutter in the wind. What does that make you think of? What does it make you feel? You look at the bark, the twists and turns in the branches. There are stories in every tree, in every living thing. We are all a part of each other."

Nancy takes another sip of wine, holding the stem of her glass with both hands now. Her lips are moist and pink.

"When I was a kid, I named all of the trees in my back-yard. Each tree had a story, a history. They were like a family. Sometimes even dysfunctional."

"Were you an only child?" I ask, realizing too late this might sound a little harsh.

"Yes, I was," replies Nancy. "But that doesn't matter in this regard. I've spent my whole life talking to the trees, to grass, to fungi. Don't people speak to their puppies and kitties? Is that considered weird?"

"You make a good point. But animals can interact with us," I say.

"The trees interact with us too. They just move in deep time. Their messages are sent over hundreds of years. They're sending messages from the future to us now, as if to say *stop doing what you're doing, human race. We don't need you, but you need us.*"

"I love the concept," I say skeptically.

"Try it some time. You'll see. Talk to the trees. Talk to all living things. Personalize all of it."

"While you guys are talking, I'll go see what Isaac is up to in his room," I say. I settle into bed with him and he puts his head on my shoulder.

"Let's read for a while. Your brain is going to turn to mush with all those video games you play."

"You always say that, Dad."

"I say it because it's true."

"How was the little cutie?" Nancy asks when Isaac's asleep and I'm back on the patio.

"He was great. You know, he asked me the usual slew of questions. How far away is the sun? How far away is the nearest star? I bored him to death and that made him fall asleep."

"What a nice dad."

"He's a good dad," Mariella says.

The lights dim.

"Did someone blow the candle out?" I ask.

Next thing I know, Mariella takes me by the hand and the night takes a new direction.

Talking to the Trees

When we get back to Brooklyn, I feel like something is changing in my mind. Since I've been reading books on trees, birds and nature, I'm noticing things now.

During our bike rides down Argyle to Prospect Park, I stop and take pictures of trees and birds. I now have an application on my iPhone that can snap a picture of a tree and tell you what kind it is.

I'm even urging Isaac and Mariella to take more bike rides.

"Let's go out. It's a beautiful day. I've been working from home all day. I'm going crazy."

I don't tell them yet, but I've begun to name trees that prominently stand out. The ones I can identify. There's Grok, I say to myself, pointing with my eyes at the live oak that stands tall and wild in Prospect Park.

I place my hand on Grok.

"Hello," I whisper. I look up at the branches. "I'm sorry if I haven't noticed you before." I close my eyes. I see images flashing across my mind: when Grok was first planted. Grok watching children play. The cars blasting exhaust in his direction. The many times I stalked by without noticing that a living creature was in my midst.

And there's Fiddle, I say, pointing at the tulip poplar standing as if on its knees in the middle of a grass meadow. Fiddle is about forty feet tall with a massive sturdy round trunk.

Looking again to make sure no one can hear me, I say, "I'm so glad you're here," adding "I'm sorry that I didn't notice you before."

I place my hand on the bark. Gazing up at Fiddle, I realize that he's talking telepathically to me. He speaks in images, not words. A single image unfolds eons of history. It's as if I'm seeing stars being born, planets forming, lives lived but all in single images strung together like sentences.

Now Fiddle sings to me a melody. If I had to translate the melody into words it would say *you humans are obsessed with your own narrow concerns. You don't see the living beings around you. The birds, the trees, and the insects. You don't feel the life that is pulsing everywhere. Just like you, we have lives. We have sorrows and joys, but we also comprehend our connection to the soil, to the animals that feed on us. To the insects that try to kill us. To the fungi, sometimes friend, sometimes foe. Even the rocks have life in them. And so we wait for you to wake up.*

I don't know how I'm able to understand so much, as if my mind has learned new languages or other ways of communicating. My two eyes, ten fingers and four limbs have boxed in the world around me. I am now opening up the lid of that box, ever so slightly and I am flooded with revelations.

It occurs to me that, when I was on that acid trip with Paul thirty-six years ago, the tree was trying to tell my *future self* something that I'm only now understanding. Or is it that my *future self* is now trying to tell my *past self* that I need to start listening to trees? That acid trip punctured a hole in the space-time fabric. A hole or a loop. Like a miniature particle accelerator nestled between my temples, the tree experience is the pivotal moment of my life. As I ponder this, a salty tear runs down my cheek. I breathe in a faint smell of sulfur.

My hand still on his bark, I thank Fiddle. My fingers tingle with heat. I bless myself like I did in school with my fingers still hot from the bark.

Turquoise Curtains

I've always lived in small apartments. Sometimes I feel suffocated but mostly I love it. Mariella designed our kitchen cabinets and living room decor. I contribute to the book collection.

Like many Brooklyn apartments, it has a sunken living room, which gives the impression of spaciousness.

The first thing you see when you enter is the turquoise-colored curtains. I would never have chosen that color, but it's perfect. The curtains are flanked on both sides by books on topics ranging from philosophy of mind, philosophy of religion, and indigenous Americans to technology, ancient cultures, and, of course, novels. The rust-colored couches are draped with Navajo blankets, Tibetan throw pillows and another pillow bearing a portrait of Aldous Huxley in the center.

Behind the curtains, on the window shelf, are statues of the Buddha, Socrates, Venus di Milo, Odin, and a glass Om stand. Our living room faces east. When the light streaks through the window, the glass Om casts a series of star-like dots on the living room walls.

The room reminds me of a genie bottle. Late at night, I slide from the couch onto the Moroccan carpet, high on marijuana, whiskey in hand, put on music and drift. I've spent hours in this position, sometimes singing along with music. Sometimes I cry. Sometimes I laugh while crying. I move between worlds. I skim. The music is like a river on which I float, dreamily conveyed by the ancient curves. I visit ghosts, entertain sorcerers, and conspire with saints here. On the surface of the music, I drift back in time and listen to Yes with Squid. We are forever young in these visions. The world is before us. Open. Infinite. My hair is thick and dark. I don't have any back pains or bodily aches. Squid is invincible; he can jump off a building and land on his feet without hurting himself. Our laughter is like the laughter of gods. No one can touch us. Sometimes I call Squid in the wee hours. He'll text me the following day. *You were hysterical last night.* My phone shows us talking from 1 a.m. to 2 a.m. *Sorry Squid. I didn't mean to call so late.*

I'll always take your call, he texts. I love Squid.

Our home is our sacred space. While I often wish for more room in this little Brooklyn apartment, I am at home here. It is my spaceship, my refuge. My UFO.

The Great River

This is a recurring dream.

I'm walking along the Great River that runs across the earth. It goes on and on, across continents. In my dream, the Great River extends beyond the Earth. I leap from submerged rock to rock. Now and again, I am washed by the Great River's terrific rain squalls. I feel the wetness on my face.

As far as my eye can see, the Great River continues. I'm going to walk on it forever, it seems. But this doesn't concern me. I feel free.

There are other people walking along the Great River. Many of whom I do not know. But we smile knowingly at each other. We are all going somewhere, although it's not clear exactly where we are going. It is good to be on the Great River. It is always summer here. A red cardinal alights for a moment a few feet away. It chirps, spins its head around, then flies away. I wish I could hold that beauty in my mind until the end of time, I think.

A few feet away, I see a man walking closer. Now in front of me, I recognize my father. But he is young. Younger than when I was a boy.

"Are you going fishing today?" he asks. "You can always find fish here," he adds.

"I don't have a fishing rod," I say.

A translucent silver disk appears in the sky above us. I look up. My father does not. He doesn't seem to notice anything. It is silent but I feel its presence heavy in my chest. The silver disk is transmitting a pulse directly to my heart. I am reminded of my father holding my hand when I was a kid. The feeling is something like love. The silver disk is now beaming a column of illuminated light in the area where I'm standing. The light gets brighter and brighter, until it seems like it's going to erupt. I am being pulled up into the light.

In an instant, the silver disk and the light vanish.

I see my father standing before me.

The sun is now blaring in my eyes. I squint so I can see him better. He's in no rush to speak to me. Maybe he doesn't know who I am, I think.

"Do you like to fish here, Dad?" I ask.

He looks sharply at me for a minute. His cobalt blue eyes sparkle in the sun.

"I only fish when I need to," he says, smiling. "But I love it here. I love that we can take our time on the Great River. We can take forever. Like you, I never noticed the birds, or the trees. I love that I can now talk with them. Don't you love that too, son?"

Hearing him say "son" surprises me. My throat gets tight. My eyes become moist.

He starts to walk away, continuing on his journey.

"Can I come with you?" I ask, clearing my throat.

"We each have to go our own way," he replies. Seeing the disappointment in my face, he adds, "but maybe we can fish together for a while."

He hands me a rod.

"I never liked fishing before, I'm different now."

My father looks young. His arms are popping with veins.

"Let's fish for now. Come, follow me," he says.

We walk together on the Great River, negotiating boulders in the water. The gurgling sounds of the river transform into the alarm sound I set on my phone when I awake.

Talking About the UFO Phenomenon

Scrolling through books online, I come across an interesting title called *The Ancient Curves*, an obscure work by an anonymous writer from the 1950s who used the name Hermes Trismegistus, after the early Greek alchemist. Admittedly, I'm drawn in by the cover, an image of a person floating upside down in space, enclosed in a translucent cobalt sphere. Like the Hanged Man. He's been spun around. Flipped.

Reading *The Ancient Curves* sets me on a journey of reading and discovery. Trismegistus connects the world's wisdom traditions with the paranormal, in the spirit of William James, Friedrich Nietzsche and Charles Fort, who had made similar observations. His writing is prophetic. And reads like poetry. I grasp for meaning in the words even as I think I understand them. Like a dream. Like I've read them before.

A new stream of books flows through our apartment door. Like water through a broken levy, new books come in floods. A wreckage of books accumulate around the house. A great flood consumes me.

Ufology, abductions, philosophy, religion, books on owls. I must paddle my way about the apartment.

"The books are beginning to pile," says Mariella, as I guiltily open a newly arrived package.

I make excuses and promises. "Don't worry, I'll get rid of some of the books." But which books can I part with? I need them all. I read them. They are my blood. I ride them on their backs like a God surfing hot lava as it pours down a mountain.

I get into discussions with friends on the topic of UFOs. They don't want to talk about it.

My dear friend of twenty years, Claire, tries desperately to avoid the topic. But I can't help it. I want to engage. After all, I need to put this book collection to use.

On Friday nights, Mariella and I often have friends over at our place for drinks. To ring in the weekend. I usually take an edible or smoke some pot. When I smoke pot, I am sometimes unable to remember the sentences I start, so I must be careful. Any topic that requires thinking can be challenging. One Friday night, emboldened by my new stack of UFO books, a few beers, and an edible, I open the conversation.

"Have you been following the reports on UFOs?" I ask.

"There's nothing concrete in the evidence," Claire says. She's very smart. But like most of the public, she hasn't really delved into the topic. I know if she does, she'll understand.

"The Pentagon released a report a year ago basically saying that they don't understand the data they're seeing. That, in the United States, and elsewhere, we have many cases of unidentified aerial phenomena," I say. "They have a video of tracking an object moving at incredible speeds. The pilots who recorded the sighting are trained observers."

Like most Americans, she hasn't paid too much attention to that report. If there is an intelligent species zooming around our airspace, the American public isn't interested. The implications are too much to bear.

I veer away from discussing the report. I should just show the TikTok clip that was published in *The New York Times*. You would think this would have caused a tremendous stir. It hardly gets any notice. Only crazy people believe in UFOs.

Instead, I go into the philosophical aspects of *the phenomenon* as it is now called.

"Science is limited because we only study things that we know. When a phenomenon occurs outside of our paradigms, we don't know what to do with that information—so we put it aside." I'm referring to Thomas Kuhn's *The Structure of Scientific Revolutions* but fail to present his argument. Maybe I should discuss these things when I'm not stoned.

"Until we get hard evidence, I don't believe these reports," Claire says. "It is my belief that science will eventually answer the unknowns and solve the mysteries of these phenomena."

There is so much of her point of view that I don't agree with, but I can't seem to articulate my point. Her use of the word *belief* is an example. We are all trapped in our own beliefs, our own worldviews.

"Our minds are limited, bound by the time and contexts in which we live," I say. "Why should the human mind be capable of understanding everything about how the universe works? We can't even understand how ants think. How trees feel and communicate. We're bloated with the efficiency of the technology that we've created. It makes us feel invincible. All knowing. But we're not. Discovery of the microchip has made us think we're gods," I add.

"I'm logical," says Claire. "I follow the facts, not conjecture."

As Claire speaks, I think of my reading of Wittgenstein, which I dare not repeat aloud. I remember Wittgenstein struggling with the nature of language: that we are trapped in our words. Our language conceals meaning, even from ourselves. And yet we can express the notion of its limitations. We simultaneously live inside and outside of language. As we grasp for understanding, we are forever chasing our tails in an infinite loop. But now, I'm feeling uncertain, like someone afraid to take a few tentative steps on the ice.

Mariella changes the conversation. Retreating into myself, I hang suspended in thought, feeling like I am standing atop a glass mountain, cold and alone.

Later that night, Mariella asleep, I sit alone on the carpet, leaning against the couch, thumbing through a book of UFO illustrations, daydreaming, drifting through the delicious silence of the night.

I Am the UFO

My imagination is renewed. I am deep in a UFO trough. There are piles of UFO books in my house. And more are coming.

"We're out of room," says Mariella.

I try to sneak the books in the house, pile them on shelves, and arrange them on furniture. I keep digging the well deeper. Understanding more. Or at least believing I'm understanding more. In *American Cosmic*, Diana Pasulka writes that perhaps *we* are the UFO. Our brains and bodies are the antennas. Our brains tune into the frequencies in which intelligent beings communicate.

Lying on my bed meditating, I explore this idea. I slow my breathing, like I always do when I meditate. This time, I use a visual as my breathing gets deeper. I imagine myself moving past the moon, then past Mars, and so forth. I see my body moving farther and farther out, beyond the Milky Way. I glide past Andromeda, 2.5 million light-years from Earth. I've left my body. I am a breeze blowing across the fabric of space. I am far, far away. I listen.

My mind is like a livewire, open. There is a silence so thick it's like the hum of a machine. I communicate with another being. A community of beings. We don't use words. It's an exchange of feelings, of images. Emotions sweep over me; chills run through my body. Sounds warble across my mind. Echoes of choir music. There is conversation. I just can't completely describe it. Words come to me, but the words are like little machines. They fit together. They're like explanations of how things work. I must stop because I'm a little frightened. Like something was getting too close. As if it might take me over. But maybe I'm just scared.

Would my father say I'm going crazy? Of course, he would. And maybe I am going crazy. But in those deep silences, there is an infinite space. However distant the beings are, we are connected. Einstein used the term "spooky action at a distance" to describe the idea that the fates of tiny particles are linked to each other even if they're separated by long distances. Perhaps this is what I'm tapping into. It does feel a little spooky. Like things you might bump into during the night. It is unknown territory. Close to the edge.

UFO Art-i-ficial Intelligence

I go through phases. I am currently deep in a UFO phase. This elicits objections from most people. And I don't always connect with people interested in the UFO phenomenon. I'm not interested in chasing down every crash retrieval or sighting. I'm interested in the philosophical aspects of UFOs: Are there other intelligent beings in the universe? Where do we come from? Are we alone? But I've always been fascinated by UFOs and spaceship designs. My mind was raised on the futurological images of *Omni* magazine, *Star Trek* and *Star Wars*.

But now we have Artificial Intelligence.

Isaac, turning twelve in a month, asks me about ChatGPT.

"Have you seen any of the ChatGPT tools?"

I haven't yet.

"Take a look here," he says, clicking a few parameters and generating a very strange image.

"Is this a free tool?"

"No, it's a trial," he says.

At my desk, I start to play with the free tool. It's interesting. Limited, but fascinating. It doesn't seem to get the human form correctly. Too many fingers, some fingers are shorter than others. Extremities are elongated and monster-like. For now.

I find an application called Jasper. I play with it, do a trial, and finally subscribe after playing around with it for a few days.

I create art based on images I upload and criteria I select. Most of the images are ugly. Or just not aesthetically pleasant to me. But sometimes I hit on one that's beautiful and unique.

I don't always remember the crazy strings of words I've used to create them. I should write them down.

I'm only working on UFO images. My focus is on the nexus between ufology, futurology, and spirituality.

While others worry about the danger of AI, I play with it like it's a fun toy. To learn from it. To have it teach me. To follow its lead. I wonder if ChatGPT's evolution will be connected to contact with non-human intelligence.

When I close my eyes, I see the UFO images I'm creating.

Perhaps because of this, I dream about UFOs frequently. In one dream I see a long string of UFOs that are connected and moving together horizontally like a cigar shaped galaxy. The first in the line of the UFOs looks like an array of bright white lamp bulbs. This is followed by a string of long pine trees lying sideways. All of this is moving across the sky slowly and powerfully. I say aloud "This is a UFO" to Mariella who is suddenly standing next to me. While I'm glaring up at the sky, I think that the phenomena is reflecting back to me the way it thinks I see it.

My friend Pinto has an art studio on Coney Island Avenue. We often meet on his roof to discuss big ideas, drink beer or whisky and smoke pot. There's a whole community of artists who stop by.

A favorite of mine from the group, Josiah, asks me, "Do you believe in UFOs?" I've been posting pictures of UFOs or UFO-inspired images on Facebook and other social media. Tall and bearded, Josiah, has a PhD in English literature and teaches at one of the New York City colleges.

"Do you mean do I believe in silver flying saucers?" I say, as I take a toke on the joint he's passed me.

"Yes," says Josiah.

"The silver flying saucer is the new chariot. The new Our

Lady of Guadalupe. The new Jesus. Or Buddha."

"That kind of doesn't make any sense," Josiah says, snickering.

Smiling, I acknowledge his laughter. It's funny. I understand.

"The flying saucer is just the current manifestation of the UFO. When Ezekiel experienced the phenomena, he saw it as a golden chariot. Today, we're technology focused. So whatever unidentified phenomena we encounter, that which we can't explain, we experience as technology. I'm sure our vision of the phenomena will morph over time. Perhaps AI will direct us towards this future vision." I trail off with a chuckle. But perhaps I'm not far off. Perhaps sentient beings will prefer to speak to our Artificial Intelligence technology, since it's profoundly more powerful than we are.

Even as we end this conversation, I know that Josiah thinks I'm full of shit. But I also know that mainstream academics—I am generalizing—are committed to the notion that the human condition is just a heap of meaningless despair. We're out here in the universe all alone, for no fathomable reason. Any glimmer of hope is an indication of ignorance. I don't want to be encumbered by inside-the-box thinking. I don't have a subject matter to protect. I want to go where my curiosity leads me. When you find yourself going down the UFO rabbit hole, it's hard to stop your momentum. Like a freight train barreling forward. You see connections between things you might have missed previously. The fact that quantum mechanics is connected to consciousness, that the mind collapses the wave function, makes my heart beat faster. Is this all a simulation? Are we some kind of experiment in a cosmic laboratory? Or is it that we just can't wrap our minds around the deeper truth of things? The second I understand something, I sink deeper into the mystery. Like mental quicksand.

Returning to Earth

Cookie falls in 2014, breaking her hip, and her mobility rapidly disintegrates. Cookie is angered by her lack of independence. It is difficult to watch.

Mom's chronic obstructive pulmonary disease, or COPD, is in its final stages. Her oxygen level is dangerously low. She has mostly been sleeping on the couch, weak. Patty, checking in on her, calls an ambulance to take her to the hospital.

When I arrive at the hospital, Mom is completely lucid, yelling at the head doctor, "What is wrong with me?"

"I need to ask you more questions," Dr. Chen, losing her patience, shoots back.

"I've been here for eight hours and you need to ask me MORE questions?"

"It's important I do a proper diagnosis."

Cookie stares coldly at her. If she could get up, she'd strangle the poor woman. "When can I see the doctor?"

"I am the doctor, " Dr. Chen says. "I need to ask more questions."

Cookie looks at me, rolling her eyes.

"Do you smoke?" the doctor continues.

Cookie appears not to hear Dr. Chen.

"She used to," I say.

"Don't EVER speak for me," Cookie barks.

I'm trying to deescalate the situation by moving the survey along. But it's only making Cookie angrier.

"Do you drink alcohol?"

"Yes."

"How often do you drink?"

"Whenever I want," replies my mother. I try not to laugh.

As this continues back and forth, it is apparent that Dr. Chen fails to manage Cookie. Admittedly, she is like a powerful giant tied to the side of a mountain. She's going to take everything down with her. But a sense of humor would help Dr. Chen handle my mom. She takes my brother, sister, and me aside.

"There is nothing we can do for her. She's in the final stages of COPD," she says flatly. Of course, we know she has COPD.

"What do we do?" asks Patty.

"Take her home. She has seven to ten days." Seven to ten days rings in my head. Over and over.

We bring Mom home to a hospital bed set up in her living room directly in front of the television. The television is her best friend and worst enemy. Sometimes it's all she has. She often shouts at me that there's nothing on television.

"Turn it off," I say.

"It keeps me company," she replies.

Cookie has been adamant that she doesn't want nurses and attendants in her apartment. And none staying overnight.

But now, after years of my brother, sister, and me, along with grandkids, taking care of Cookie, alternating days and nights, bringing her food, and keeping her company, we need professional help. This is what normal people do. There's no other way.

When the nurse visits, Cookie accuses my sister of planning behind her back. As if she's plotting. As if we're all plotting. "I know what you're doing," she says, glaring at Patty. "And you're in on it, too," Mom adds, looking at me. "Get the fuck out of here," Cookie shouts at the nurse, who smiles and helps my sister change her anyway.

The nurses and attendants offer very good care information. How to turn her. How to change her. Administer the meds. But her health continues to decline. She's often sleepy and sometimes forgetful.

Day ten comes and goes. Mariella and I take turns with my siblings staying over at Mom's. We have the nurses and attendants come during the day, but we don't want Cookie to wake up to a stranger. It might confuse her and it would scare the hell out of the attendant.

At 27 days, she wakes up and asks for coffee. She hasn't had coffee in a few days. My siblings and I administer the pain medicine: morphine and methadone. Between fatigue and nervousness, I don't feel competent measuring the dosages.

"I want to have coffee at the kitchen table," Cookie says.

Mariella and I look at each other.

"How am I going to get you to the table?" I ask.

Cookie thinks for a bit.

"That's right. I can't walk," she says. Like it's just occurred to her.

"Here's what I'm going to do," I say. "I'm going to bring the table to you."

"OK, do that," says Cookie.

Mariella and I lower the table attached to the hospital bed as Mom looks on dreamily. I bring her coffee in a sippy cup.

"No, this isn't my coffee cup," says Mom.

"I didn't want to spill it; this is easier to drink." Mariella and I hold the cup so it won't spill on her. Cookie takes a few sips and starts to talk. She looks past us, beyond us, to someone or something else.

"There's a woman dressed in red. She's dancing. She's alone. A man comes up to her."

Playing along I ask, "Is the man handsome?" I follow it up with more questions. Cookie answers them. She's seeing something we aren't seeing. After a few minutes, she abruptly asks, "What's with all the questions?" Like her old self. Almost immediately, she falls asleep. That's the last conversation I have with my mother.

Next shift: Patty and her husband arrive. Mariella and I leave. On the drive home, I get a call from my sister.

"You have to come back. Mom is shaking and trembling. She's talking incoherently."

My siblings, along with their spouses, are circled around Cookie. No one speaks. Cookie shakes her head, gesturing and mumbling. Every so often I hear her say "fucking" or "friggen." She's in a state called hyper-agitation, we learn from the nurses. Her body seems smaller, shrunken. Maybe she'll get smaller and smaller until she disappears. Her face is blurred and flickers at the edges.

Cookie looks through you when you look at her. Her eyes glaze over. Sometimes her glance moves away from your face to something else she's seeing—a memory or a drama playing out. She's dreaming. She reaches out to touch something. She makes sad faces. Even scared faces. Sometimes she smiles. Her personality, at times, manages to bubble to the surface of the deep well she's in.

When she stares through me, I feel like she's looking directly at my soul. Her eyes have become crystal balls. Images from the past float across their opalescent surfaces: the time I snuck into my parent's bedroom at night and stole Mom's favorite diamond ring and sold it. The lies I've told. Times I've left her sick and alone, knowing she wanted me to stay, but I was tired. I had to go home after six or seven hours. Two, three times a week.

And take the interminable train ride from Queens to Brooklyn. Arriving home irritable.

"She's transitioning," one of the nurses says. "She's not ready to go yet."

Cookie wrote in her will that she didn't want to be kept alive artificially. She's been unable to eat food for a week. Her body is eating itself. Turning her over to wipe her backside is painful for her. Her legs are stiff and rigid, her body like a wooden board.

"Why is Mom's skin blotchy and bruised in places?" Patty asks.

The nurse says her organs are dying. "In a day or two her bones will break through her skin," the nurse adds.

Patty and I sigh. "Oh my god." I feel sick. This is dizzying. We plead with her. "Mom, it's OK, we understand that you need to go. We love you, but we don't want you to suffer." This is very difficult to watch unfold.

Later that night, I recite Catholic and Tibetan prayers for the dying.

"I commend you, Mom, to Almighty God, and entrust you to your Creator. May you return to Him who formed you from the dust of the earth. May holy Mary, the angels, and all the saints come to meet you as you go forth from this life. May Christ who was crucified for you bring you freedom and peace."

Somehow Patty and I, perhaps the most ill-behaved kids of the three of us, are the ones leading the prayers. Seeing my mother in this in-between state is emotionally intense and puts me directly in contact with the limits of my humanness. I feel each breath moving slowly in and out of me—wind sweeping through my bones. There is a line between death and life just as there is a threshold before birth. Each state has its own rules, its own horizons. Perhaps seeing the lines blur yields a kind of wisdom.

We say prayers late into the night, then take turns sleeping. I head to sleep at about 2 a.m. Patty stays up with her husband and Mariella. When I wake up at about 6 a.m., Cookie has passed. I don't cry. I feel a fathomless gloom that is too deep for crying.

After the burial, I walk away thinking that we're leaving her there in the dirt all alone. No one to turn the television on or off. No one for her to call. Her body is now returned to the Earth. She is no longer ours.

At the funeral luncheon, I look down at carrots, scallions and peppers that came from the same earth where my mother is, where I will eventually be. A body in the dirt, a meal for living things who will likewise crumble into its bosom.

The Light Around Us

Through the window in my bedroom comes the sound of trees ruffling in the wind. The wind beats against the window glass as if to say *let me in*. Mariella is fast asleep but I can't sleep, the noise rattles my nerves.

Rising out of bed irritated, I walk towards the window. I see a bright beam of light shining down on the street outside my apartment building. From here I can't see its source.

"What's going on?" Mariella says, woken by my rustling.

"I don't know. There's a bright light outside. I'm going to check it out," I whisper.

"Now?" she asks.

"I'm curious. I'll be right back."

"Hurry back, I'm cold," she says, shrugging her shoulders, pushing her face into the pillow.

I slip into a pair of pants, skipping on one foot, put my shoes on one at a time and stumble out the door. The street is empty. Middle of the night. Parked cars. Silent. An owl hoots in the distance, probably in the nearby park.

The beam of light is so bright it's hard to look at. Straining my eyes, I see that its source is an object hovering about two hundred feet in the air. My eyes begin to tear; the smell of sulfur fills the air. Although the beam seems pointed at a particular spot, the sidewalk is flooded with illumination. It's quite beautiful. I am reminded of Moses's burning bush. I'm not at all afraid or concerned, although I'm usually a worrywart. I am certain that this isn't a police pursuit. Otherwise, I'd hear choppers roaring.

I hear only the wind wildly shaking the tree leaves. After a brief silence, the sky goes completely dark, like everything has been sucked up into a vacuum of empty space.

As if a lamp has been turned on, I see a brilliantly lit disk hovering above the trees. Its light showers down on me. I am overjoyed by the sensation of power that the disk emits. In my awe, I almost get to my knees to pray. The disk, the UFO, is the most powerful entity I have ever encountered. Although soundless, its power is palpable, like it could lift the Earth and fling it into space. From what I can tell the UFO is perhaps twenty-five feet across. And yet, I can only think that it is like the sun, massive, inexhaustible. There is knowledge in the cascade of light that pours down from it.

Suddenly the light stops. I look up quickly and notice that the UFO has become a shadowy blot in the sky, as if its immense light source has folded inward. In less than a few seconds, it moves horizontally at an incredible speed and disappears. No sound. My eyes still fixed on the night sky; I see a light appear among the few viewable stars. Could it have gone that far that fast?

A train roars past, startling me. We live a block away from the tracks. We mostly don't hear it, but in this silence, it sounds thunderous, like a spaceship taking off.

Still gazing up at the sky, I see a bluish white light wobbling and swelling, then shrinking and growing again. This repeats in a loop. Whatever it is, it looks like a pulsing organism. Although far away, it seems to rush closer to me. It's in front of me, like it's waiting. Like it wants to communicate with me. I carefully reach out to touch it. Its exterior ripples when I press my index finger on it. I see swirls of deep blue and white light swimming on its surface. I swear I think it's laughing. I start to giggle. The swelling light tugs at me with something like a gravitational pull. It's gentle. I feel it walking me over to the window in my apartment building. It moves my bedroom window slightly up. Standing on my tippy toes I see Mariella fast asleep, but when I look again, I am curled up next to her. A wave of shock washes over me. Am I dead? Am I dreaming? I take a deep breath, trying to remain calm. Perhaps I can direct this dream now that I am awake in it.

The light lifts me up and slides me into the thin opening of my window. I am being transported by a beam of light. Floating around my apartment, I see my eleven-year-old son, Isaac, sleeping in his room. His red lips are pursed as he breathes. The blonde ringlets of hair on his head drape across his face, like tree leaves. He looks peaceful, like he always does when he sleeps.

Whatever is dragging me is pulling me along by my hand. I don't seem to be in control. I am stopped at my bookcase. As I peer at the titles, my books seem a little silly. The topics range from philosophy to science to literature.

I think I hear the light giggling again. I don't know what else to call it.

"What?" I ask. "Do you find my books funny?"

I hear laughter in my head. Not a mocking laughter, but more of a titter.

We're not laughing at you. We're laughing with you.

So now I'm talking to myself, I think.

No, you're not talking to yourself. We're all talking together.

Why are you laughing at my books?

We admire you. In fact, we love you. You put so much faith in your books, you're learning, and yet you know so little.

"Am I insulting myself?" I say out loud.

It is a laugh of love. Of kindness.

Suddenly, I'm not in my room anymore. I am in a whirlpool of light and bright colors.

"Where am I?" I ask.

You are in another realm. That realm is in your bedroom. You just can't see it, normally.

I pick up one of my books, *The Ancient Curves* by Hermes Trismegistus. On the cover is a man in a spacesuit. When I open it, I see words, but also corridors of mathematical equations that jump off the page horizontally. As I turn the pages, I see various scenes play out, as if I'm watching a film. I see a body of water. I'm swimming through the water. It's bright blue. Schools of albacore and swordfish pass by. Giant plumose anemones flutter with the ocean waves. My heart slows down as I take this all in. I can feel myself changing shape, dissolving. I see myself, but I am not me. I am a soft blue coral, pulsing and swaying in the water, waiting. My mind is no longer mine. I am thinking in a manner that resembles warbling color. I'm not sure if that even makes sense. My thinking doesn't map to words, or at least not to words I know. The only comparison I can make is that I am thinking in time and space, or like I am thinking in music.

This scene evaporates.

Have you read any of this in your books?

I'm still recovering from whatever it is that I've just experienced.

There are things all around you that you don't understand.

I'm still holding *The Ancient Curves* in my hand.

Turn another page, the light says.

I behold incredible three-dimensional visions that contain emotions and longing, mixed with joy and wonder.

In one chapter, a movie plays the history of my life. It is not chronological. Layers of my history intersect with other events, other phenomena. Going to first grade, I wear the bowtie my parents insisted on. Its metal wire captures my attention. I'm drawn into its story. How it was made in a factory. Its constituent components. How it was melted together in a vat. The workers who poured the heap of metals into the vat. Each thought races to a deeper place of understanding. There are infinite points of diversion. For a moment, I see them all, like I'm flying over the Earth in an airplane thirty thousand feet in the sky.

I'm holding the book again. I flip it over in my hand. The book is not just a collection of pages. It is a living thing. Everything around me is alive. I'm just usually blind to all of this.

Exactly, says the light. *You are blind to all of this for the most part.*

"Why?" I ask.

We don't know. We are like you. We are a part of you. This is a mystery to us as well.

"How do I visit these places?"

You are here all the time. Slow down. Don't think with your mind. Think with your heart. Talk to the trees, to the grass. Even to the stones. You are them as much as they are you.

"I'm not sure I understand. I do a little bit, but just for a moment and then I don't."

My attention turns back to the book. I open it again and see a page that shows my dead body in a box below the soil. I hear music brushing over me. It is a string symphony sung by the wind. There are other sounds, too. The sounds of trees growing. Of grass tittering in the wind. An owl hooting. I feel myself stretching, elongating. As if my feet are wound up in the mycorrhizal loam that interweaves the soil. I am dead, but I am also alive. I'm both. As I look closer, I see my face as a young boy, then as an old man, older than I am now. My face transforms into my father's, then into my son's face. I weep at the passing time. Memories disintegrate like dust. Holding my son's hand is like my father holding my hand. How did I not notice this before?

I am struck by a sudden darkness. My body in the soil grows cold and damp. I'm lonely until spring, when a meadowlark alights on the grass above the ground. Its melody is sweet and sad. The song is wise, telling of the many lives that are lived by all creatures, all beings. The song urges us not to dwell on melancholy. When we awake to understanding, we see that those we miss are still with us. In fact, we are them. The songs connect us, wrap around us, and interweave our concerns, hopes and fears. The song is us.

I am back in my room. The light has subsided. I am me again. I am very tired.

"What was out there?" asks Mariella, not opening her eyes.

I sit on the bed beside her, taking off my shoes, then pants.

"It's a long story. It might take me a lifetime to explain. Let's talk about it tomorrow."

I snuggle up next to her. It's still dark out. But there is a shimmer of light outside our window.

Acknowledgements

This book was made better by all who read iterations of it before my work went to the publisher.

I am grateful to the many reviews and inputs that I received from my wife, Arielle, my son, Thelonious, and my friends, Susan Kaessinger, Angela Welch, Sam Mastandrea, and Bill Bernthal. And thank you to Nancy Graham for providing additional editorial oversight. I am also grateful to MK Barnes for her assistance in bringing the book to life.

I am likewise indebted to Dr. Diana Pasulka, Dr. Jeff Kripal, Rob Dickins, Joshua Cutchin, Anthony Peake, Pricilla Stone, Dr. Jack Hunter, Alan Steinfeld, Marla Frees, and *Perceptions Today*, for their readings, support, and insights.

About the Author

Mike Fiorito is an author and freelance journalist. His book *Falling from Trees* won the 2022 Independent Press Distinguished Book Award. Mike's other books include *Mescalito Riding His White Horse*, *Sleeping With Fishes*, *The Hated Ones*, *Call Me Guido*, *Freud's Haberdashery Habits*, and *Hallucinating Huxley*. For more information, please go to MikeFiorito.com.

Apprentice
House Press
Loyola University Maryland

Apprentice House Press is the country's only campus-based, student-staffed book publishing company. Directed by professors and industry professionals, it is a nonprofit activity of the Communication Department at Loyola University Maryland.

Using state-of-the-art technology and an experiential learning model of education, Apprentice House publishes books in untraditional ways. This dual responsibility as publishers and educators creates an unprecedented collaborative environment among faculty and students, while teaching tomorrow's editors, designers, and marketers.

Eclectic and provocative, Apprentice House titles intend to entertain as well as spark dialogue on a variety of topics. Financial contributions to sustain the press's work are welcomed. Contributions are tax deductible to the fullest extent allowed by the IRS.

To learn more about Apprentice House books or to obtain submission guidelines, please visit www.apprenticehouse.com.

Apprentice House Press
Communication Department
Loyola University Maryland
4501 N. Charles Street
Baltimore, MD 21210
Ph: 410-617-5265
info@apprenticehouse.com • www.apprenticehouse.com

Printed in the USA
CPSIA information can be obtained
at www.ICGtesting.com
JSHW010306220124
55616JS00010B/165

9 781627 205269